Mason shrugged. "As a crime scene, it doesn't make a lot of sense. I'm beginning to suspect the killer of providing too many motives for his crime."

"To sum up, then," said Amirah, "we don't know why Kadeem Nassar was killed, other than it probably wasn't in order to rob him. On the other hand, we do know the killer has to be someone who was familiar with Kadeem's schedule, to know he'd be in the parking garage around six-thirty last night. And thanks to Sa'id, that's not all we know."

She related the latest information her cousin had gathered from the victim's laptop. "He was able to trace which server the three threatening emails originated from. Well, not the exact server, but at least the general location of it. It came from a server in Canfield Tower, the home of CanCorp, where Kadeem just happens to have been working as an auditor for the last two months."

Mason raised his eyebrows and Vaughn whistled softly.

"You're talking about the Canfield Corporation," he asked, "that massive brokerage firm downtown?"

Amirah nodded.

"Wow. You guys are swinging in the big leagues now…"

# No Accounting for Murder

## by

## Darin &
## Sarah Fortner

*A Gates & Gates Mystery*

**No Accounting for Murder**

Cover Art by *Lea Schizas*

The Wild Rose Press, Inc.
PO Box 708
Adams Basin, NY 14410-0708
Visit us at www.thewildrosepress.com

Publishing History
First Edition, 2023
Trade Paperback ISBN 978-1-5092-5204-6
Digital ISBN 978-1-5092-5205-3

Published in the United States of America

Chapter 1

Kadeem Nassar was concerned, even a little worried, but he wasn't afraid. Perhaps if he had been, he might have lived through the night.

It was just after six o'clock on a Wednesday evening, and the main thought on his mind was that he was still hungry. He had been out with friends for dinner and drinks a little earlier, but the restaurant had been too trendy, the meals too expensive and the portions too small, and he had come away unsatisfied.

He was back in his apartment now, and after only a moment's debate, he opened the refrigerator and pulled out a plate of his mother's *samboosahs*, leftovers from family dinner the previous weekend. He thrust the dish into the microwave and jabbed at the timer. In his opinion, even four days old and nuked, they beat nearly anything else he could imagine.

When the machine beeped, he carried the plate around the kitchen island and into the living room. As he settled down in front of the television, he reached for the remote with his free hand, and his eyes automatically went to the cell phone resting beside it on the left arm of the sofa.

Emails hadn't been checked that day, even though it was his normal routine to scroll for texts and other messages as soon as he got home. He had to look sooner or later, though. He couldn't avoid it forever.

He forced his attention back to the flat-screen television mounted above the imitation fireplace and flipped through the streaming service menu, but got only ten or twelve minutes into the movie before finding himself staring at his cell phone again. He had to know.

He put down the half-empty plate and the remote and picked up the phone. The first two emails in his inbox were from family, the next a payment-due reminder, and then there it was.

It was from an address he'd never seen before he started this latest job, and now he'd been contacted three times. Just as on the other occasions, the subject line was blank, and the message was brief and to the point.

THIS IS THE FINAL WARNING. NO ONE WANTS YOU HERE. QUIT BEFORE IT IS TOO LATE.

He blinked at the screen. What should he do? Take the threats seriously? Explain the situation to his boss and resign from the job?

No.

Growing up Saudi-American in the shadow of 9/11, he'd experienced his share of slurs, intimidation, and abuse. He had never let other people's foolish prejudices stop him before, and he wasn't about to start now. Besides, how great a risk was there that the person who was sending these messages would actually act on them? It was true, Cathedral City had its share of violent crime, like any city of its size west of the Mississippi, but it was rare to hear about that sort of thing happening in the financial district, where he lived and worked.

He took a deep breath, shut the phone off, placing

it back on the arm of the sofa, and resumed watching the movie.

At 6:20 his phone beeped at him. He scooped up the remote and swiped at the phone's screen to shut off the alert. Two evenings a week he set aside for a light workout at the gym, just to keep in shape–more than that didn't seem necessary, for a reasonably active twenty-two-year-old.

He changed into his exercise clothes, grabbed his gym bag and a bottle of water from the refrigerator, then headed downstairs. His apartment building was one of the oldest ones in its neighborhood, and lacked any in-house exercise facilities. His gym, however, was only a six-minute drive away–ten minutes if traffic was heavy. And he made up for his laziness in driving there by skipping the elevator and jogging down the four flights of stairs to the basement parking garage, thereby getting a head start on his workout.

He had made up his mind. He wasn't going to be scared away from his job, but he was going to tell his boss about the threats, and whatever happened after that was out of his hands.

He pushed through the exit door at the bottom of the stairs and stepped out into the dimness of the garage, heading for the space that held his sports car. He had a bright red 2011 Toyota Supra, a little on the flashy side but old enough that his father had not disapproved too much when he co-signed the loan. As he came around the driver's side of the car, he realized that something was wrong with it.

He stopped with his key fob in his hand and leaned forward to get a better look.

Someone had scratched the paint. Not a small

scratch, either–there were marks across both the front and rear doors. He bent down further and ran his finger over the grooves.

They weren't just scratches, and it wasn't accidental.

Someone had taken a thin blade and gouged two words into the side of his car.

His eyes widened at the message. Straightening up, he bumped into the black Volvo in the next space as he stepped backward.

That was as far as he got. As he came level with the rear bumper, there was a sudden movement behind him, and before he could react, an arm wound around his throat, immovable as an iron bar. He clutched at the arm with both hands, grappling and pulling, but it was no use.

There was a second swift motion, and the last thing Kadeem felt was a stinging pain as the small, thin blade slid into his heart.

Chapter 2

Leila Nassar was at home when the news came about her brother.

Her home was a Tudor townhouse in the Vesper Downs subdivision north of the city, on the other side of the river. In actuality, it was her parents' home: at the age of twenty-four, and after having completed a four-year business program in community college, she still lived with them, in the room she had grown up in. This was not by choice or from economic necessity, but solely due to her father's decree. Despite emigrating from Saudi Arabia in the mid-nineties with his pregnant wife to escape the increasing violence of the fundamentalists, Abdullah Nassar was in many ways a traditional Saudi father, and in his household, his daughters were to stay at home until a suitable husband was found for them. His sons, meanwhile, had been provided with a small allowance to live on their own as soon as each of them reached twenty-one.

Dinner was over, and the three of them were relaxing in the family room. Abdullah, a stout man with a salt-and-pepper beard, was sitting comfortably at one end of the sofa with his hands folded across his middle, intent on the game show playing on the television. His wife, a relatively petite woman in a loose blouse and capris, the sort of outfit she favored around the house, worked on her embroidery at the other end of the sofa.

Leila was sitting cross-legged in her cargo pants in an armchair, her attention primarily on her phone.

The doorbell chimed unexpectedly. Her father jabbed at the remote to silence the TV and stared wordlessly at Leila and her mother, then began to rise.

"No, *baba*," Leila said, putting down her phone. "I'll get it."

She strode through the house to the front door and opened it cautiously. They were not accustomed to having strangers show up on their property unannounced, and family members would have had the courtesy to phone ahead.

Two men stood on the porch. The one in front, who couldn't have been much taller than Leila (no more than five feet five inches or so, surely), looked as if he'd stepped out of an old movie, with a three-piece suit in black pinstripe, a matching snap-brim hat, an electric blue paisley tie, and gleaming black leather shoes. What struck Leila more than his ensemble, though, were his stony blue eyes. The second man, taller and lankier than the first and standing slightly behind and to one side of him, was dressed in nothing fancier than a sports coat over a polo shirt, and his expression was weary.

"Yes? Can I help you?"

The man in the three-piece suit asked, "Is this the home of Abdullah and Fatima Nassar?"

"Yes…"

"Can I ask who you are, miss?"

Piqued, Leila replied, "I think I should ask the same thing."

The man in the snap-brim held his wallet discreetly at waist level and opened it to display a silver badge.

"My name is Detective Arthur Jensen, CCPD. This is Detective Quint. Are Mr. and Mrs. Nassar at home?"

Leila's heart rate rose. "What's this all about?"

"There's been an incident. It'd be better if we stepped inside to discuss it, don't you think?"

She opened the door unwillingly and stood back to let them enter. Her parents had come into the entryway by then, her mother hanging back a few paces behind her father. Abdullah gestured to the left and led the men across the spacious hall to a sitting room decorated in bright colors and bold patterns, the room in the house reserved for guests. They took the places offered to them on the plush maroon loveseat, while Nassar sat uneasily in a large leather wingback chair and his daughter drew up a high-backed ottoman.

His wife hovered in the doorway and asked uncertainly, "Should I bring coffee for our visitors, Abdullah?"

Jensen shook his head and removed his hat to reveal a barren scalp ringed by a fringe of close-cropped black hair. "Nothing for us, ma'am. If you'll come in and sit down, please?"

Once they were all seated, Jensen re-introduced himself and his partner and said, "I won't beat around the bush. We're here to bring you unpleasant news, and there's nothing I can say that will soften it. It's regarding Kadeem Nassar. He's your son, is that correct?"

"What has happened?" Abdullah asked, gripping the arms of his chair. "What has happened to Kadeem?"

"When did you see your son last, sir?"

"He was here on Saturday for family dinner. We have not seen him since then, but he sent us a text message on Monday and yesterday."

"Was he in the habit of carrying much cash on him?" asked Quint.

"A small amount, for emergencies. Fifty dollars, a hundred dollars, maybe a little more."

"Credit cards?"

Abdullah stared at the lanky detective, and then at his sharp-dressed partner.

"He has two that I am aware of. A young man his age–" He stopped and asked again, more forcefully, "Will you tell us what has happened, please?"

Jensen cleared his throat. "Roughly two hours ago your son was attacked and robbed in the parking garage of his apartment building. I'm sorry to have to tell you, he didn't survive."

There was a lull while the Nassars processed what they had just been told. Abdullah drew in his breath sharply and squeezed the arms of his chair even more tightly, like a man in danger of falling off a cliff. His wife whimpered and clapped her hands over her mouth. Leila felt her head spinning.

Her father began, "There must be a mistake–"

Detective Jensen stood, followed by his partner, and placed his hat back on his head. "No, sir, I'm afraid there's no doubt about what happened. Your son's driver's license was still in his wallet when it was found. However, I will need one of you to come to the medical examiner's office to make a formal, legal identification."

Abdullah, in a daze, started to rise from his chair, but Jensen waved his hand.

"There's no need to do it tonight. You're going to want some time to take this in. If you could come down in the morning, though, it would be appreciated. Here's my card, and I'll write the address of the ME's office on the back for you. Give me a call when you're on your way, and I'll have someone meet you there."

With that, the two detectives were gone, leaving the Nassars standing in their guest room in bewildered silence. Leila went to her mother and slipped her arms around her, laying her head on her shoulder.

There were no tears that night, and not much conversation. Leila supposed her parents, like her, were holding on to the slim hope there'd been a mistake, that any moment Kadeem would call or text, and tell them he was just fine.

In the morning, she insisted on going with her father to the address Detective Jensen had given them. A brief flurry of discussion followed. Abdullah, in his turn, insisted that someone needed to stay there with her mother, and since Leila was the only child still living at home–

Finally he acquiesced, seeing that he was getting nowhere. Leila called one of her aunts to come over right away, and then phoned the police headquarters to let Jensen know they were leaving.

Leila drove them in her little car. The trip passed in almost complete silence. She wanted to reach across and take her father's hand, for his sake and for hers, but he was not normally a demonstrative man, and she was half-afraid he would reject the gesture.

They headed south across the Carey E. Kefauver Bridge, the most direct route from their neighborhood into the heart of the city. The online directions she'd jotted down took them past the downtown commercial section to a medical district blanketed with buildings, most of them university-affiliated. After winding around the complex, they arrived at a sparsely-populated parking lot in front of an uninspiring concrete building. The blue-and-gray sign in front of it read TASKER COUNTY MEDICAL EXAMINER AND FORENSICS.

Detective Quint was waiting for them just inside the metal doors, wearing the same faded blazer and camo-patterned canvas shoes he had had on the previous evening.

Leila expected to experience something like a scene from a TV show, with a dramatic unveiling of a sheet-covered body on a metal table in a chilled room, but what happened was nothing like that. They checked in at a grilled reception window, then Jensen led them down a corridor to a small cubicle that could have been a visiting room in any of a thousand doctors' offices, complete with a worn metal desk and some uncomfortable plastic chairs. After a short wait, an older black man wearing a white coat and a sympathetic expression came in, said a few words to them, and then, taking a seat behind the desk, turned the monitor of his computer around so they could see it.

There on the screen was Kadeem's face: the apple-shaped jawline, the slightly tousled black hair, the notch of an old scar tissue at the corner of his left eye. His eyes were closed, and only the odd background and the lack of color in his skin gave any indication that he wasn't simply asleep.

The sight of that little pink crescent beside his eyebrow brought back the memory of an eight-year-old Kadeem, excited to try out his brand-new bicycle, hurrying out of the house the morning after his birthday and pedaling down the drive toward the street. The pavement had been damp with pre-dawn rain, and before he could correct his course or brake, he had run face-first into their mailbox. Leila had been the first to reach him and had wrapped her arms around him while he sobbed and bled onto her shirt.

Leila squeezed her eyes shut, but the sudden tears leaked out anyway.

Abdullah swallowed, nodded, and managed to get out the words, "Yes. That is my son."

He signed and initialed the form placed in front of him, and it was over.

"Thank you, Mr. Nassar," said Quint. "We'll get your son's personal effects to you as soon as we can."

The detective gestured vaguely and they followed him into the corridor. The three of them were turning the corner, heading for the exit, when the second blow of the day came.

Abdullah was saying, "You understand, Detective, we must have my son's body returned as soon as possible, to properly prepare him for burial."

"Of course, sir, but there'll have to be an autopsy first—"

A brown-haired and bearded man who was leaning against the reception window, chatting with the attendant, pushed away when he caught sight of them. "Kadeem Nassar's family, by any chance?"

Abdullah slowed his steps and responded stiffly, "I am his father."

"John Skokos, *Sentinel-Gazette*. Mr. Nassar, do you have any comment on the death of your son?"

He held a small digital recorder out to them. Abdullah Nassar waved it away.

"I have nothing to say to you. Please, leave us alone."

"As a member of the Arab-American community of Cathedral City, are you surprised that your son was targeted in a hate crime?"

Detective Quint thrust out his arm and brushed the reporter to the side, none too gently. "They said they don't want to talk to you. Do I need to repeat that?"

"Hate crime?" blurted Leila. "What are you talking about?"

The reporter ignored Quint's long, outstretched arm and answered her promptly.

"Haven't the police told you–Miss Nassar, is it? The killer scratched the words 'Die Arab' into the side of Kadeem's car."

Leila's eyes widened and her breath caught in her throat. She flashed a look at Quint, but the detective, his expression blank, did not meet her gaze.

Chapter 3

Mason Gates lifted his eyes over the upper edge of his newspaper yet again and reflected that one of the advantages of being a husband was that he was free to admire his wife whenever he felt like it.

She was standing a few feet away with her back to him, energetically making breakfast in the kitchen of their ranch-style home, clattering dishes and spoons and humming some current tune he couldn't name, completely unaware that he was contentedly running his eyes up and down her bare legs. The sunlight slanted through the half-opened blinds onto the round table in their breakfast nook where he sat scanning the headlines, and the scents of fresh coffee and frying meat mingled with other, fainter morning smells.

He had risen first, out of long habit, and had taken the time to shower, shave, and dress fully before stepping outside to pick the newspaper up off the driveway. She, on the other hand, had climbed out of bed in her sleep shirt and had yet to put on any other clothing. That was one of the unexpected details he had discovered after they were married, that if given the opportunity, she was content to wander around the house in the most minimal of attire.

He had no intention of complaining.

Amirah Gates was five feet four inches–about average height for women in her family, it turned out–

and pleasingly curvy. She was a dozen pounds or so shy of being plump, and he had on one or two occasions called her *"zalabia"* teasingly–Arabic for "dumpling." He had quickly learned that it was not a term she was fond of.

He eyed the hem of her sleep shirt, which hung just below her bottom, and the backs of her thighs where they disappeared beneath the fabric, and thought about how he'd enjoy seeing even more of her. If, for instance, she needed to reach something in the cabinet directly above her, she would have to go up on her tiptoes and stretch, and her shirt would necessarily lift along with her arm and display the thin neon-blue material covering her backside...

The food was cooking away just fine, however, and her feet stayed firmly planted on the floor. When Amirah carried their plates over to the table a few minutes later, she saw the expression on his face and said wryly, "I don't think your morning coffee has kicked in yet."

She sat their plates down, yogurt and toast for her and bacon and eggs for him. With her upbringing, she would never have dreamed of eating pork herself, but after five years of marriage, she had at least become comfortable fixing it for her husband.

"Anything interesting in the paper?" she asked.

It was one of Mason's few quirks that, despite relying heavily on his smartphone for his business and carrying it everywhere he went, he still preferred to take the time to peruse the newspaper each morning for the latest headlines. He covered the first page over breakfast, and possibly the second and third pages depending on the events being described, and then carried the paper off with him to work to graze on it little by little throughout the day.

"Oh, the usual. Heat wave in India, Russian jets invade Estonian airspace, a senator convicted of corruption, more debates over whether the presidential election was rigged..."

She looked at him tenderly. At thirty-four, he still had a tidy, athletic figure, thanks to regular sessions in the exercise room at the far end of the house. His keen eyes were a light blue-gray, and his wavy, medium brown hair was kept close-clipped. There was a faint cleft in his chin, and a mole in front of his right ear. All in all–at least in her opinion–he had more than a little resemblance to a younger Ben Affleck.

"So not a single thing, huh?"

He grinned at her, lifting one corner of his mouth, as he tucked his paper away and picked up his fork. "Heard any more from your sister?"

"Not in the last twenty-four hours."

In just over a week, Amirah's parents would be celebrating their thirty-fifth wedding anniversary, and from the month's beginning, she had been receiving calls and texts at odd moments from her sister Aziza. She was perhaps half an inch shorter than Amirah, and stockier, and as the oldest of the four siblings, she expected her opinion to carry the most weight. Their other two sisters managed to "miss" her calls and "forget" her texts most of the time, so it was left to Amirah, the youngest, to weather her constant advice and suggestions.

"Her latest idea," Amirah said, "was to try to convince *mum* and *baba* to have their party at the Lotus Room, out at the Moreton Arboretum. My sister Yara talked her out of that one. Not that it isn't a beautiful location, but our father would never go for something that extravagant, let alone that costly…"

"Oh, I know. He doesn't believe in spending one cent more than he needs to."

Amirah laughed. "Are you saying my father is a cheapskate?"

"Not at all. It's one of the things we agree on. He and I both appreciate the value of a dollar. Now don't you think you'd better go get ready, before our employees start wondering where we are?"

She swallowed the rest of her toast and stuck her tongue out at him before heading for the bedroom to dress.

They lived in a newer development on the far side of Lake Womack, a man-made body, which sat at the northwest corner of the city, fed by the Manuette River and its tributaries as they snaked down from the north. Their normal drive into work took them across the hydroelectric dam that capped one end of the lake and supplied three-fourths of the power for the area. On that bright summer morning, the dam gleamed whitely in the sun like a plaster saint, and the shining water was already dotted with sailboats. To the right, they had a view down the Lower Manuette Valley, with the river surging among the sandstone formations that had given the city its name.

When they reached the bluff on the opposite side, Mason turned left onto Winter Avenue, which spanned the city and eventually brought them to the street where the strip mall holding their business was located. Their discreet suite of offices was nestled among the nail salons and secondhand shops, with dark Roman blinds covering the windows and a blue-and-black sign bearing the legend GATES AND GATES INVESTIGATIONS.

They pulled into one of the employee spaces behind the business and went inside. As they came down the corridor toward the front office, their receptionist, Cecilia McMurphy, poked her head around the corner at them, her green eyes wide.

"There you are!" she blurted out. "Goodness, I thought I'd have to call in the National Guard to track the two of you down!"

"It's only two to nine," Mason pointed out with a faint smile. Their physical location was open during standard business hours, nine to five, though Cecilia came in earlier than that to get a head start on answering machine messages, emails, and assorted paperwork.

She was a tall, skinny girl of twenty-two who dressed for the office, in Mason's estimate, rather like a librarian. She alternated between neutral tones and dark ones, kept her heavy blond hair pinned up with plain hair sticks, and wore mid-thigh open-front cardigans that only accentuated her length. The one feature which hinted at her having a more vivid style in her off-duty hours was her heavy-rimmed cat-eye glasses.

She was also a worrier.

"That's fine for you to say, but I didn't know when you were going to show up, and I didn't know what I was going to do if you didn't. You have a client," she explained abruptly.

Mason raised his eyebrows. Apart from delivery men, it was rare to have people visit their business in person that early in the day.

"I unlocked the front door at eight forty-five, like I always do," Cecilia rattled on, "and I barely had time to turn around when she came in. I hadn't even had time to get a pot of coffee going."

"Well, let's not keep her waiting!" said Amirah. "Give us a couple of minutes and send her in."

They went on around the corner into the room Mason used as his office and had only just managed to settle in, Mason behind his desk and Amirah in a chair beside it, before Cecilia swung open the door and ushered in their visitor.

"Leila Nassar."

The young woman who entered could easily have been one of Amirah's sisters, or at the very least, her cousin. Both were Saudi-American and approximately the same height, though the platform wedges Leila wore made her seem taller. She was slimmer than Mason's wife, too, in face and body, and her glossy black hair was shorter and swept up in a chic cut. Her eyes were the expected dark brown bordering on black, while Amirah's were a far rarer pale hazel. Her clothing and accessories were expensive without being overly flashy: a ruffled yellow strapless blouse dotted with tiny black flowers, light orange slimline ankle pants, a tan clutch hardly bigger than a paperback novel, and around her throat a narrow silver-and-onyx necklet.

As she took the seat they offered her, Mason wondered what her impression of them was. Certainly, they didn't look like the popular conception of private investigators, even though he still tended to carry himself like the cop he had once been. If anything, they looked like the owners of a construction firm or some other blue-collar business: Mason was dressed simply, in a navy polo and khakis, while Amirah was only slightly more formal in dark slacks, a bright primary-colored top with a rounded bolero over it, and sensible shoes of faint plaid.

"What can we do for you, Miss Nassar?" he asked.

In answer, Leila took her phone from her clutch and flipped through the pictures on it, finally holding it out to him with a photo on the screen of three young men, arms around each other's shoulders, grinning at the camera.

"The one on the right is my brother Kadeem. He–" She stopped, swallowed, and continued. "He was killed Wednesday night in the parking garage of his apartment building. Someone stabbed him to death. They–they…"

Leila's voice caught in her throat, and she fought to bring her breathing back under control.

Mason gave her a moment, then said kindly, "We're sorry for your loss. Please, go on."

Leila nodded. "His killer–his killer took all the money he had on him, and his credit cards, and left him there to die. And then, before he left, scratched a message on the side of his car–'Die Arab.' The police think it was just a robbery, that Kadeem was the victim of some random mugger who happens to hate Middle Easterners. But they're wrong!"

"What makes you say that?" Amirah asked.

"Yesterday afternoon, when my cousin and I were at his apartment to pack away some of his belongings, I took a minute to look through his laptop, just to…just to hear his voice again, in a manner of speaking, you know? And I came across three emails he'd gotten before he died, all from the same person, threatening him."

"He didn't keep his laptop locked?"

"Password-protected, you mean? Oh, yes, but he had all his passwords written down, just in case…"

"You haven't gone to the police with this information, have you?" guessed Mason.

"What's the use? They're convinced it's an open-and-shut case. The officers in charge of the investigation weren't even going to tell us about the message on Kadeem's car. A reporter told us." Leila turned her head and stared Amirah in the eye. "Do you know how many private detective agencies there are in this city? I did a web search. Fifteen. There are fifteen. I could have gone to any one of them, but I didn't. I came to you because you're one of us, and I trust you to find out the truth about who killed my brother."

Cathedral City was a decent-sized metropolis, but the number of Saudi-American families in it was small, and they comprised a close-knit community. In that circle, everyone knew of Faisal Bukhari, the restaurateur, and his daughter Amirah, who had declined a place in the family business to marry a Caucasian and become a private investigator.

Mason folded his hands together and leaned forward before his wife could respond. "We're willing to take your case," he said, "but there are some things you have to understand. We aren't the police. We can make a citizen's arrest, but only under certain limited circumstances, the same as anyone else. The best we can do for you is to compile a detailed file on your brother's murder, listing every available piece of evidence and naming the most likely person responsible. But the police aren't obligated to act on the report we give you, no matter how well the facts seem to fit together."

"That's fine," Leila blazed, holding herself stiffly upright in her chair. "If they refuse to do anything about it, we can take the case to civil court and get a judgment against the killer that way."

Mason smiled faintly at her determination, and after she had completed the paperwork he held out to her, he nodded decisively.

"Thank you, Miss Nassar. You've just hired Gates and Gates Investigations. Now, if you don't mind, let's back up and start from the beginning." Mason opened a tab on his computer, ready to start entering notes as they talked. "Your brother was killed Wednesday night?"

"Yes. Just before six-thirty p.m."

"At his apartment building, you said? Where is that?"

"The Farquhar Building, in the downtown area. 110 Van Buren, apartment 5E."

"You mentioned he was killed in the parking garage. Was he just coming home, or on his way out?"

"He was headed to the gym. Kadeem worked out twice a week, on Wednesday and Saturday evenings."

"How many people knew about his gym routine?"

Leila sighed. "I don't know exactly. All his friends, I'm sure, and everyone in our family... Maybe the people he worked with?"

"Okay. Now the killer took the cash and credit cards from his wallet. Was there anything else taken?"

Leila shook her head. "If there was, the police didn't mention it."

"And the message left on his car was scratched on it? Not spray-painted?"

"No, scratched, they said."

"There were no witnesses to the crime?"

Leila made a helpless gesture. "The police haven't told us much of anything. I don't know."

"That's all right," Mason said soothingly. "That's why you hired us. Now about the email threats. There were three of them?"

"Yes. Oh, that's something that could be important. The threatening emails weren't in his regular inbox, the service he used for family and friends. I found them among his work emails. Those go to a different address."

"Where did he work?"

"Certified Accounting Associates. They're located on Monroe Avenue, I think. He'd been working there about two years. Kadeem was always good with numbers, even as a kid…"

"You had no idea he'd been getting threatened before you saw the emails? He didn't mention it to his friends or anyone else?"

"Not that I'm aware of."

"Was that normal for him, to keep things to himself?"

Leila thought for a moment and then admitted, "Yeah, at times, I guess it was… He was like any guy his age. On the hardheaded side, wanting to tackle all his problems without asking for help…"

"Did he have any friends he was particularly close to? A best friend, maybe?"

"Oh, Daoud. Yes. I have his number in my phone, I think… Just a minute…"

"What about a girlfriend? Was he seeing anyone at the moment?"

Mason noted the names and telephone numbers as Leila located them in her contacts list, as well as getting her cell number, and leaned back in his chair.

"That's everything for now, Miss Nassar," he said. "We'll start looking into this today and let you know as soon as we have something definite to report."

He rose as she did, and after shaking their hands, the young woman departed.

"All right!" said Amirah, thumping her small hands, balled into fists, against her thighs. "Where do we start first?"

Mason couldn't help but smile broadly at his wife's enthusiasm, but settled back into his chair before he responded.

"A division of labor might be our best plan," he said. "Since I have a contact in the ME's office, I could take a look at the crime scene and then try to find out what the autopsy showed–if it's finished yet. That would give us something to start with, at least. How about you pay a visit to Kadeem Nassar's workplace, and see if you can pick up anything there, since these threatening emails seem to be connected with his job. No, on second thought, it might be better to get ahold of Kadeem's laptop, and get it over to your cousin Sa'id, to see what he can make of it."

Sa'id Alharbi, the son of one of Amirah's mother's sisters, was the agency's official "tech consultant," and dealt with anything too sophisticated (or time-consuming) for them to tackle.

"You know," Amirah said, making a face at her husband, "I can handle more than one task at a time."

Mason laughed. "Who am I to say you can't? Here, let me just make you a list of every single thing we need to look into…"

Chapter 4

Amirah inched her car carefully into the space labeled "2 Hour Parking," switched off the engine, and took a deep breath.

Despite her earlier confidence when talking with her husband, now that she was on her own, her nerves were starting to get to her. This was going to be a big case for their agency, she could just feel it. What if the people she talked to didn't take her seriously, seriously enough to give them the information they needed to solve Kadeem Nassar's murder? What would she do if they failed Leila Nassar?

Although everyone who knew her family understood the basic facts of her work as a private investigator–something which her father's friends all looked down on as an unfit occupation for a woman– most of them were unaware of the details. She and Mason had met during her last year of college, when he, a special investigator with the DA's office, was looking into a crime ring suspected of operating out of a nearby fraternity house. They had dated for two years before getting married, and afterward, he had continued on the police force while she put in part-time hours doing clerical support at her father's business. However, Mason had grown unhappy with the constant overwork, the red tape, and the judicial inequities, and when, one evening, he had off-handedly mentioned quitting the police and opening up his own agency, she'd urged him to go for it. He and a fellow officer had pooled resources to start what was then simply Mason Gates Investigations. After twelve months, Amirah, bitten by the private eye bug, talked him into taking her on in the agency as well.

That had been a year ago. Since then, she had discovered, to her disappointment, that commercial investigatory work was for the most part routine and unexciting. Eighty percent of the cases they handled–a figure that held true for most private agencies–were from insurance companies concerned with potential fraud. Other jobs they had undertaken included process serving, tracing people who had skipped out on court appearances or child support, and that old standby, gathering evidence on cheating spouses.

This was different.

The Nassar family, and by extension every person in the community who had a Middle Eastern background, was depending on them. They couldn't just accept the police department's determination of what had happened. They had to dig, and keep digging, until they'd uncovered everything they could about the circumstances of the killing.

To do that she needed to come across as professional as possible.

It would help if her heart would stop thumping in her chest–or at least come down to a manageable level.

Already that morning, she had visited the Nassars at their home in Vesper Downs, to see if Kadeem's parents could add anything to what his sister had already told them, and had taken possession of the victim's laptop and deposited it with her cousin for analysis. Now she was on the outer edge of the downtown district, preparing to interview some people who might be a little less cooperative.

She gripped the steering wheel, lifted her head to stare into the large hazel eyes that looked back at her from the rearview mirror, took another deep breath, and stepped out of the car.

The building where Kadeem had worked was a moderate-sized office block with chocolate-colored awnings on the street level and a polished but empty lobby. She studied the metal panels installed beside the elevator and then jabbed the button.

When she emerged onto the fourth floor, she headed down a thinly-carpeted hallway past a series of small business suites until she came to a sign reading CERTIFIED ACCOUNTING ASSOCIATES LLC. The office on the other side of the dark brown door was unimpressive, with simple, somewhat dated furniture and paintings of flowers in broad, irregular strokes hanging on the walls.

The bowtied black man seated behind the reception desk–somewhere between his early thirties and early forties, she couldn't quite tell–raised his head as she entered and asked politely if he could help her.

"I'm looking for Terrence Plant. Is he in?"

"Is he expecting you?"

"No." Amirah took a business card from her purse and handed it to him. "I'm here to ask him some questions about Kadeem Nassar."

The man glanced at the card, looked her over carefully, and then pushed himself back from his desk without a word and carried the card around the corner into an interior room, limping slightly as he went. He returned with a second individual, a short and stocky white man with his thinning hair slicked back and bifocals on a chain around his neck. A faint aroma of Old Leather swirled around him.

"George says you're here about Kadeem?"

"Yes, Mr. Plant. Our agency–"

The shorter man turned to the taller. "Put the 'Out to Lunch' sign on the door, George. It's early, but we can afford a longer lunch break than usual today."

Amirah had apparently caught them between customers. Plant gathered his other employee, a woman named Lynda whose torso was encased in a thick sweater covered with cat silhouettes (not to mention a noticeable number of black and white cat hairs), and led them all into his office. He dropped down heavily behind his desk, which was cluttered with papers and folders of various colors, and when they were all seated, he regarded the detective somberly.

"What's this about, Miss?" Noticing her wedding ring, he added, "Or is it Mrs.?"

Amirah smiled and nodded for him to go on.

"Anyway, Kadeem didn't show up for work yesterday morning, and when I tried his phone it went to voicemail. I called his emergency contact number around nine, his parents' home, and they told me he was killed in a mugging Wednesday night. I've been in here working my way through the personnel forms and other things… It's a tragedy, but I'm not sure what you expect us to tell you."

There was an additional question behind the man's eyes that he wasn't asking. Amirah swallowed to try to take the cottony taste out of her mouth and reminded herself to sit up straight.

"The family has hired us to look into his death," she said, "because there are indications there may have been more involved than just a mugging. We're hoping you can provide some background details about Kadeem that could head us in the right direction."

It took a moment for Plant to respond. "Oh, my... Well, in that case, just tell us what you need, and we'll be more than glad to help."

"To begin with, how long had he been working for you?"

"Just over two years." Plant exhaled heavily. "This is a small business, as you can tell, and I pick my employees very carefully. I've always tried to choose people who not only have the skills needed, and really want to be in this line of work, but who will also work well with us. We're a family here, I like to think, and from his first day, Kadeem fit right in. He was willing to learn, and he picked things up quickly, and he wasn't arrogant or standoffish. He was a young man, of course, so he could be boisterous sometimes, but I never had any problems with him."

Amirah glanced at the other two employees. "Would you say the same, that you never had problems with him?"

George and Lynda both responded quickly and affirmatively. Amirah's instinct, watching their faces, was that they were telling the truth. Wherever Kadeem's trouble had originated, it wasn't with the people at the accounting firm.

"What prompted you to hire him?" she asked. "Was it as a replacement for someone else?"

Plant regarded her steadily with his pouched eyes. "I know what you're thinking, and it wasn't that. Zella, the woman who was here before him, gave notice after learning she was pregnant for the third time and deciding she'd rather take a job that let her work from home. There were no hard feelings on that count."

"Did he ever mention troubles in his personal life? Disagreements with people he knew, threats against him, things like that?"

Plant shrugged. "Kadeem seemed like a typical, carefree young man, as far as I could tell. His family is in investment banking, so he didn't have any concerns about money, and I got the impression he was popular enough with the opposite sex…"

"Did you ever have problems with customers due to his being Arab-American?"

Plant raised his eyebrows in surprise. "I never had a single person say a word to me about that, and if they had, I'd've shown them to the door. His parents being from the Middle East didn't have anything to do with how well he did his job."

"Had anything changed in his life recently, say about two months ago?"

Amirah dangled the question like an attorney in a courtroom, hoping to get a telling response, and she was not disappointed. George and Lynda exchanged glances and then stared wordlessly at their employer, who avoided meeting their eyes. With his gaze on the papers piled on his desk, he replied, in too casual a tone, "What makes you ask that?"

Amirah took her phone from her purse and flipped to her email inbox. Before leaving the victim's computer with her cousin, she had had Sa'id forward the three suspicious emails to her, so that she'd have them within easy reach. Her first inclination was to simply read the messages to his coworkers, but she remembered what her husband had said to her since his days working for the district attorney's office, that one of an investigator's best tools was the careful control of information, and she gave them a brief summary instead.

"Around a month and a half ago, Kadeem received a short, threatening email. Two weeks ago he got another, and yesterday morning he got a third, all of them sent by the same person. By last night, he was dead. It seems like a little more than a coincidence. He didn't mention these threats to any of you?"

Plant, his eyes downcast, only shook his head sadly, while his employees once more looked fixedly at him.

"No," Plant responded at last, lifting his head. "He never said a word. Why on earth wouldn't he've told me a thing like that?"

Disregarding the rhetorical question, Amirah asked, "Does the address jjohnjohnson@mcmmail.com sound familiar to any of you?"

Her audience shook their heads blankly. She was not surprised, seeing how Kadeem had kept silent about the emails, and in any event, the sender's name was clearly a pseudonym.

"So," she asked briskly, "what happened two months ago? From your reactions, it's clear that something occurred then, and that something could very well be crucial to our investigation."

"Now, we can't be absolutely certain it has anything to do with his death…" Plant said wafflingly.

"These threats," Amirah said, "were sent to his business email, not his personal one.

KNassar98@caallc.com–that is his work email, isn't it?" There was no response from any of them, so she went on. "Whoever was threatening him is someone who met him in a professional way. And since you all assure me he had no problems in this office…"

Plant continued to hesitate, and Lynda, glaring at her employer, blurted, "Two months ago, Kadeem got a new assignment, something outside the office. We saw him maybe once a week after that. The whole thing was very hush-hush top-secret. Kadeem wouldn't tell us what it was he was working on, and Terry changes the subject every time we ask him about it."

Plant threw his short, pudgy hands in the air. "That was part of the agreement for our company to take the job. The client insisted on absolute confidentiality, for their name to be kept completely out of our records and not mentioned to anyone. I can't help it. I'm obligated to honor their request!"

"Come on, Terry!" George said, shaking his head. "I don't care what the client said. Kadeem's dead, and if you know something that can help…"

"He's right, Mr. Plant," said Amirah. "I understand the need to respect a client's wishes for privacy since it comes up in our business as well, but I think in this case circumstances outweigh anybody's wishes. Someone purposely killed Kadeem Nassar, and if the work he was doing has even the slightest bearing on his death, we owe it to his family to find that out, don't you agree?"

Plant sighed and lowered his gaze to his desk. "All right. I give up. I can't argue with that… Two months ago, I was contacted by the head of the accounting department at CanCorp, requesting someone to assist with a full-scale, company-wide audit. They wanted someone who was computer-savvy and who could concentrate solely on their project to the exclusion of everything else. I immediately suggested Kadeem. I never imagined…"

"CanCorp?" Amirah repeated. Despite her best efforts to keep a professional expression, she felt her pale eyes go wide. "You mean the Canfield Corporation? The multi-state, billion-dollar brokerage firm?"

"That's right. You can understand now why they requested me to keep it quiet. If it became public knowledge that they'd called in an outside company to help perform an internal audit, then confidence in the firm would plummet, stockholders would start bailing, and before long they'd be fighting to stay solvent."

Amirah nodded, but her expression was distracted. "What I wonder," she mused, "is why a company that large felt the need to hire an outside auditor at all?"

Chapter 5

The Farquhar Building, where Kadeem Nassar had lived and died, was located on the western side of the business district, not so very far from where Amirah was at that moment, just a block or two off Logan Avenue as it zigzagged along the cliffs that made up the city's west boundary. It was a tall, narrow structure of pale yellow limestone in the Second Empire style, the oldest luxury apartment building in Cathedral City. The term applied loosely: as the years had gone by, the luxuries had become less luxurious, while the rental prices had remained relatively high, and the white-collar offices which flanked it had been replaced by downscale establishments like tanning salons and pawn shops.

Mason parked across the street from the lobby and strolled around the corner to the entrance that sloped down into the Farquhar's basement garage. There was an attendant on duty in the parking booth, a young man with curly black hair who appeared to be of mixed Latino and black descent. The nametag on his short-sleeved brown uniform said MARCO.

"Can I help you?"

"I'd like to talk with you about what happened here yesterday evening."

The young man shook his head. "You can't be a cop, because I talked to a dozen of them yesterday. So you must be a reporter, and I don't have time to talk to reporters. Besides, there's strict rules about non-residents being down here."

Mason took his card from his wallet and held it out. "I'm not a reporter–and you're right, I'm not a cop, either. I'm working for the Nassar family, helping them find out exactly what happened to their son. You can understand that, can't you?"

Marco stared at the business card and sighed. "Yeah, I wouldn't want to go out like that and my folks not know what'd happened to me or why. Okay, fine, I'll tell you as much as I can–but I still got to do my job, you know? Besides, I don't really know all that much about it."

Mason smiled. "I'll try not to get in your way. Were you here when it happened?"

Marco shook his head again. "No, that was the other parking attendant, Mr. Robles. His name's Cayetano, but everyone calls him Chuck. Everybody but me, I mean–my mamma raised me to be respectful. We work twelve-hour shifts here, six to six. I have the day shift; Mr. Robles has the night shift. It happened about half an hour after he came on duty."

"Did he see anything? I suppose the police asked him a hundred questions about it."

"Something like that, yeah. No, he didn't see it go down. He was in the booth here when one of the residents came tearing around the corner, yelling that there was a dead body and he needed to call 9-1-1. It had to've happened after his shift started–first thing we do when we come on is walk the garage, make sure nothing's been stolen or damaged during the previous shift. If one of the residents was stretched out on the garage floor, Mr. Robles would've noticed."

"And Kadeem Nassar was dead by the time he got to him?"

"Yeah. Before he called the cops and got our boss on the way, he checked for a pulse, but there wasn't one. He said it was funny because there wasn't much blood and the body was still warm, but Mr. Nassar was stone dead."

"Did Mr. Robles see or hear anything suspicious just before it happened?"

"He swears he didn't. The cops took him into our boss's office, and had the two of them play Wednesday's security tapes for them, but I guess there wasn't much to see. It sounds like the killer slipped in through the lobby and then took the emergency stairs down here to the garage and headed for Mr. Nassar's car. I guess he kept close to the outside wall, kind of in the shadows."

"How hard is it to get into the lobby? Can just anyone do it?"

"Sure, anybody. That way the mailmen and delivery men can get inside to the mailboxes. You can't get onto the elevator without entering a security code, though. The emergency stairs are another matter. Fire safety regulations, you know."

"What about the killer's appearance? Did you hear anything about that?"

"From what Mr. Robles said, there wasn't much to go on. The guy had a black hoodie on and kept his head down and his hood up the whole time. They didn't get a clear view of his face from any of the cameras."

"I understand the killer took all the money from Kadeem's wallet before he fled the scene."

"Yeah, that's what I heard."

A dark blue Lexus swung into the garage, and Marco broke off to confer with the driver. She accepted his offer of valet parking and glanced at Mason as she emerged from the vehicle. He smiled blandly at her. The driver was a short woman in her mid-fifties, with frizzy brown hair the same color as the Pomeranian she was clutching in her arms, and she did not smile back. She nodded curtly and warily at him before making a wide circle around him and headed for the elevator.

When Marco returned, Mason asked: "Was Kadeem in the habit of carrying much cash around with him?"

"I guess he was. He always tipped me well."

"And that's something anyone who knew him would know? Friends, family, other tenants?"

Marco shrugged. "I guess so."

"Did you ever chat with him when he had a spare moment?"

"We talked some now and then. Discussed the weather, TV shows, music–stuff like that. He wasn't much older than me. Had to been the youngest tenant in the building. I think he probably just liked having somebody his age who knew what he was talking about."

"Did he ever mention any personal problems? Or talk about being threatened?"

Marco stared at him. "No, man, nothing like that. He seemed like a regular guy. I mean, being Middle Eastern, he probably had people hassle him sometimes, but he never mentioned it to me. I guess that's the kind of thing he'd talk to his own people about, you know?"

"He never had issues with anyone in the building?"

"Not that I heard of."

A second vehicle rolled into the garage—a white sports convertible, and the offer of valet parking was declined. The car pulled into a space about halfway down the length of the building and its occupants, a middle-aged man in a bright polo shirt and chinos, and a young blond woman in a floral jumpsuit, stared at Mason as they crossed the garage floor.

"Did Kadeem ever mention his work to you?"

"Nah. I got the impression he did some kind of tech job, but it ain't my place to ask the tenants about their personal lives."

"What did you think when you heard about the message scratched into the side of his car?"

Marco shrugged. "Not much to say about that, is there? Whoever killed him had a problem with Muslims. Lots of people got a chip on their shoulder these days, always hating on somebody else."

"The parking spaces here–are they marked with the residents' names, or just numbered?"

"No, just numbers."

"Do you mind if I take a look at the spot where it happened?" Mason asked.

"I guess it's all right. It's number twenty-three. But try and make it quick, man. I don't need the tenants complaining about a stranger hanging around the garage, not after what's happened."

Mason smiled. "I understand. I won't be long."

Although the garage took up the entire basement of the building, the area available for parking was L-shaped, with the primary section around the corner from the entrance, as the attendant had indicated. Kadeem Nassar's Toyota Supra was still in space 23, cordoned off with stanchions and police tape, leaving the slots on either side of it empty.

Mason stepped up to inspect the message scratched into the driver's side of the car. The letters had been cut into the paint with something narrow, possibly the tip of a key or more likely the weapon that had been used in the murder, so that a person had to be standing fairly close, or under strong lighting, to read them clearly. He narrowed his eyes and shook his head.

He paced back and forth for a few minutes until he was satisfied he had located all the security cameras that had a view of that section of the garage, and then returned to the booth at the entrance, where Marco was finishing parking a burgundy BMW.

"One more question before I go," he said. "Have there been any unusual incidents around the building lately, anyone hanging around in areas they shouldn't have been in, things like that?"

"Not that I've heard. I haven't noticed any strangers around, but you can bet I'll be keeping my eyes open now."

"Good," Mason smiled and handed the young man the rectangle of cardboard he had shown him earlier. "Why don't you hang on to my card, and if anything happens, or you hear anything or remember anything important after you've notified your boss and whoever else you need to, give me a call. It'd be appreciated."

"You got it, chief."

Chapter 6

Mason Gates let the man in the lab coat and pale scrubs look around the restaurant for a moment before calling out to him. He didn't have to raise his voice much to catch his attention—he was sitting at the first table inside the entrance.

"Right here, Jeff."

The man turned in his direction. "Mason! You've already ordered?"

The detective nodded, and the newcomer headed for the counter. He returned after several minutes, having made his way through the line and stopped off at the soda fountain, carrying a plastic tray. On it were cellophane-wrapped plastic utensils, including chopsticks; a plastic marker stamped with a large, brightly colored number; and a tall cup of sweet tea.

They were seated at an inexpensive, cafeteria-style Thai Fusion restaurant called NuVang, on the northeast side of the sprawling medical complex that neighbored the ME's office. The tiled dining room was furnished with square, chocolate-topped formica tables and plastic seats in various colors, while posters of assorted South Asian locales hung here and there on the walls.

"What did you get?" Mason asked.

"The pad thai, of course. You know it's my favorite. What about you?"

"The beef khao pad. I haven't tried it before, and

the picture on the display looked inviting."

The man opposite him chuckled. "Now, you're a big boy. You know how it is with menu photos. If it isn't everything you thought it would be, don't expect anyone to sympathize. Although it can't be too disappointing, not here."

Mason's fellow diner was Dr. Jeffrey Scanlon, tall and slim with wavy blond hair that was just beginning to recede around the edges. Scanlon was one of the assistant medical examiners for the county. There was a faux-leather planner tucked under his arm. He extracted a buff file from the planner and opened it.

"I suppose we'd better get down to it since this is the price I have to pay for you to ask me to lunch. I know. It's too much to think that you'd foot the bill for nothing more than old times' sake. And the sooner I get this file back to the office, the better, since I'm not strictly authorized to take it out of the building in the first place…"

The two of them had known each other since Mason's days on the force, having become friends fairly quickly after their first meeting. Mason grinned.

"Let me know if they decide to execute you, and I'll bring the blindfold. It's the least I can do."

Scanlon made a face at him. "Now, I didn't have a hand in this particular autopsy, so I only know what's here in black and white, but I'm certain it's as thorough as it should be. Urakawa conducted it, with Blassing as her assistant, and it would be rare for her to miss something even remotely important."

The server appeared and placed ceramic bowls of food on their trays. Mason's bowl held stir-fried rice with strips of beef and assorted vegetables in a sweet chili sauce, while Scanlon's had a heaping pile of rice noodles with bean sprouts, peanuts, and bits of egg seasoned with a savory sauce.

Scanlon propped the opened file to one side and began reading between bites.

"Kadeem Abdulrashid Nassar, age twenty-three... I don't suppose you need to know height and weight and all those incidentals... Subject deceased approximately three to four hours before the start of the examination. Cause of death was a single stab directly to the heart, immediately beneath the sternum at an upward angle–which it would have to be, obviously... The instrument was a single-edged blade around five cm in length, razor-sharp and fairly narrow... Only the tip of the blade reached the heart, but it was enough to do the job. The lower edge of the wound was ragged, which suggests that the base of the blade was at least partially serrated.

"Apart from the fatal injury, there were various small cuts and abrasions on the victim's face from landing on the concrete floor of the parking garage where he was found...

"Ah, there's something else here. There was a faint bruise on the left side of the victim's neck, from a point just under his left ear to a point above the laryngeal prominence–his Adam's apple," Scanlon added in explanation.

"So. Conclusions?"

Scanlon leaned back and took a long swig of his sweet tea before answering.

"You know from experience how this game works, Mason. We gather all the facts we can from the cadaver and make our report. It's up to you investigators to draw the inferences and find the evidence and the suspect that fit the facts. Having said that, I suppose the first scenario we could imagine would be unintentional... The assailant was arguing with the victim, or attempting to rob him, and the confrontation escalated and he ended up stabbing him, without any intention of actually committing murder..."

Mason shook his head. "That's out, for a couple of reasons. What else have you got?"

"I didn't believe it myself, to be honest. All right. The bruise on the victim's throat would tend to make me think the assailant struck from behind and grabbed him in a chokehold before stabbing him. Seems pretty intentional in that scenario."

"Any way of determining if the killer was right- or left-handed?"

"I can take a guess–just an educated guess, mind you–but from the bruise on the throat and the angle of the wound, upward and slightly to the left, I'd incline toward the theory that the killer restrained his victim with his right arm and delivered the blow with his left hand. If you want to be sure of that, though, you'll have to talk to Dr. Urakawa."

Mason nodded. "A single strike directly to the heart–could that mean the killer has some kind of medical background?"

"It's possible. It could be someone with training in anatomy. Or your killer could be someone in the military, or someone who's taken a lethal force self-defense course... This is why you invited me to lunch, isn't it, so you'd get a good straight answer?"

Mason chuckled. "Straight, hmm? Remind me never to let you do carpentry. And the weapon? Any chance it was something medical?"

Scanlon raised his eyebrows. "A scalpel, you mean? Going out on a limb on that one, aren't you? No, the shape of the wound doesn't really fit. A scalpel has a rounded blade, whereas this weapon had a straight edge –and a serrated base, don't forget. A small pocket knife, maybe, or the killer used something like a hobby knife or utility knife for God knows what reason…"

Mason prodded at his fried rice, thinking. "Do you have a list of the victim's belongings there?"

"Yes, there's an inventory from the crime scene. Looking for anything in particular?"

"Or something that isn't there, maybe. I don't know. Go ahead, read."

Scanlon nodded. "Dark gray T-shirt, Adidas track pants, briefs, athletic socks, navy tennis shoes, white Fitbit watch, silver OnePlus smartphone, key fob and three keys on a keyring, black leather wallet with driver's license, social security card, Selective Service card, Aetna medical insurance card, key card, Herschel gym bag containing a change of clothing and a bottle of water."

"No money?"

"Not on this list. No cash, no credit cards. I'm presuming his assailant took those."

"It appears that way. The gym bag hadn't been rifled through?"

"Doesn't sound like it. The bag was zipped shut when the Crime Scene Unit arrived, and it contained everything it should have: polo shirt, jeans, spare socks and underwear, towel and soap, deodorant, a bottle of Glacial water."

"Hit and run," Mason muttered thoughtfully.

"That's right. Robbery ending in murder. Just another day in Cathedral City."

"Except the circumstances don't jibe. There's something more behind this killing."

"Well, you know your business." Scanlon gulped down the last of his pad thai and pushed his chair back from the table. "It's been great sharing a meal with you, Mason, but I'd better get this file back before anyone misses it."

Mason gave his friend a grateful smile. "Thanks, Jeff. I'll take your check, too. Lunch is on me."

"Oh, it most certainly is, pal."

Chapter 7

The early afternoon sun gleamed so strongly off the freshly-graveled lot and the vehicles on it that Amirah fumbled for her sunglasses as she lowered her car window.

"Daoud Hassan?"

The young man leaning against the trunk of the green Hyundai saw her eyeing the nametag on his striped work shirt, which read something else, and nodded. "You can call me Dave. Everybody outside my family does. You're the private detective?"

She nodded and switched off the engine. They were in the employee parking area behind Palladin Logistics, a trucking firm in the southeastern section of the city. Kadeem Nassar's sister had named Hassan, who worked on the loading dock there, as his closest friend. Amirah had called the number Leila had given her just before lunch, and when the young man didn't pick up, she left a message identifying herself and asking him to contact her as soon as possible. Fifteen minutes later, she received a text telling her to meet him in the parking lot behind his work at two-thirty, the time of his first afternoon break.

Hassan was on the tall side for an Arab-American, with a long face framed by a wispy beard and mustache. His chest, as well as the arms folded across it, were well-developed. He was, she had to admit, easy on the eyes.

"Like I said in my message, our agency's been hired by Kadeem Nassar's family to look into his death. You've heard about that?"

"Yeah, his mom called my mom late last night and gave her all the details. It was some kind of hate crime, wasn't it?"

"That's one possibility. Do you have time to talk? I don't want you to get in trouble with your boss."

"Sure. I told my team leader I'd need a longer break than usual. They know what happened, so I think he'll cut me some slack."

"I've been told you and Kadeem were close."

"We've known each other since we were in elementary school," Hassan said. "I mean, we knew each other–" He shook his head and stared off into the distance. "It doesn't seem real, you know? I know it is– I saw the headline this morning–but part of me keeps thinking I'm going to be getting a text from him any time now, asking what I want to do this weekend."

Amirah nodded sympathetically. "It takes a while for it to sink in. Did Kadeem talk about his personal life much? Perhaps something he said could give us a hint to lead us to his killer."

Hassan gazed back to her. "What's to say? Of course, we talked about the things going on in our lives, everyday stuff. I never imagined something like this would happen to him."

"Did he mention any problems he was dealing with lately, at work or elsewhere?"

"No. I thought everything was fine with him."

"Did you know he had been receiving threatening emails?"

Hassan stared at her with widened eyes. "He was? You're sure?"

"I've seen them myself."

"And he never said a word to me about it. I can't believe it. Why wouldn't he tell me? We told each other everything."

Clearly, Amirah thought, that wasn't the case.

"How long had he been getting these emails?" asked Hassan.

"They started about a month and a half ago. They may have something to do with a project he was working on. Did he talk about his work much?"

"No, but then, I didn't really talk about mine with him, either. Neither of us has what you'd call exciting careers. He was an accountant, for crying out loud. It isn't exactly a non-stop thrill ride."

"He didn't mention any particular assignment he was working on recently?"

Hassan frowned at her. "Is that what got him killed? Something to do with his job?"

Amirah, picking up on the young man's skeptical tone, said, "Unless you can think of something else that changed in his life recently?"

"I'm not sure, all right? But when I heard about Kadeem, and the message on his car, it got me thinking... He started dating this girl about three or four months ago–"

"Harper Ashby."

"You know about her?"

"Only her name and cell number, so far."

Amirah had tried to contact Kadeem's girlfriend after interviewing the Nassars, in fact, but had only gotten the young woman's voicemail, and as yet there had been no response to the message she had left for her.

"Yeah, I don't know much more about her. Where she works, that's about it."

"Oh, yes? Where's that?"

"Concierge Realty. It's somewhere in the Winwood area."

"I see. So, what did you start to say about her?"

Hassan took a deep breath. "Okay. I was out with some friends a while back at a club and I happened to see her with a guy, having a pretty intense discussion. Black dude, real dark, with a shaved head and a leather jacket. The kind that looks like he's got a beef with the whole world. Not really my business, but then, not too long ago, we were at that same club and I spotted the two of them again, still going at it. I started asking around, to find out what was up. Turns out he's her ex-boyfriend. His name's Antoine or Anthony, something like that, and he's the jealous type. Apparently, he's been trying to get back together with her, and he was giving her a hard time dating somebody with a Middle Eastern background.

"When I heard what happened to Kadeem, and the message his killer left, it made me wonder."

"How long ago was this, the first time you saw the two of them together?"

"About two months ago, maybe. I don't remember exactly."

"And the second time?"

"Just this past weekend. Saturday night."

Amirah was silent for a moment, digesting this information. The timing seemed to match up with the timing of the threats Kadeem had received, but she wasn't entirely convinced the two were related. There was something about the phrasing of the emails that made her doubt a jealous lover had sent them. On the other hand, what if the emails were simply a coincidence, and had nothing to do with the murder?

"So," she said, "you think her ex had seen Kadeem and Harper together at this club, or somewhere else?"

"He must have. I'm pretty sure it's her favorite club, and it's where she and Kadeem met."

"The name of the club?"

"Tesseract, in Mannheim."

The Mannheim district was a trendy uptown quarter, where bohemian artistic types rubbed elbows with the children of moneyed families. Chances were this ex-boyfriend, however he dressed and acted, was more upper-middle-class than gangsta.

"The real question," Amirah said, half to herself, "is how he could have gotten hold of Kadeem's work email… Well, we'll look into it. Is there anything else you can remember that you think we should know?"

Hassan shook his head. Amirah took a business card from her purse and held it out to him.

"If anything occurs to you, anything at all you think might help, call our office right away."

He stared at the card and then at her. "You're going to find his killer, aren't you?" he asked hopefully.

"We're going to do our very best. Trust me."

After a quick call back to the office to check in and get some directions from Cecilia, Amirah drove north to the Winwood section of the city. Concierge Realty was a one-story building of dark brick and tinted glass on a relatively quiet street. When Amirah stepped into the carpeted lobby, the first thing that caught her eye was the girl behind the reception desk, a plump young woman with a mass of bright carrot-colored hair and faint freckles across her cheeks and nose. The girl, with a bored expression, had her head down and was scrolling through posts on her phone.

"Harper Ashby?" she asked, stepping up to the desk.

The girl lifted her face in surprise. "Yes?"

Amirah took a business card from her purse and held it out discreetly. "I'm working for Kadeem Nassar's family, and I was hoping to talk to you about him. You do know about what's happened?"

Harper shot a glance at the door to her boss's office and hissed, "I can't talk to you here. This is where I work!"

Amirah put her business card away and said quickly but firmly, "Why don't you take a break and come see me outside? I'll be waiting in my car, a tan Civic."

It was almost thirty minutes before the girl emerged from the building and looked around. Amirah, watching her in her rearview mirror, tooted her horn, and Harper trotted along the sidewalk to her car, her stiletto heels clicking on the concrete.

Amirah watched her as she climbed into the passenger seat and wondered if under her conservative pin-striped charcoal business suit she had one or more tattoos and piercings.

"Look," the girl said anxiously, "you just can't come here like this and start asking me questions! I'm going to get in real trouble with my supervisor! If he finds out I was dating Kadeem, and now I'm involved in a murder case…"

Amirah felt the heat rise to her cheeks. Her first impulse was to apologize, but then she reflected that Kadeem Nassar was dead, and finding out who was responsible was worth a little inconvenience for the people who had known him.

"You're not going to get in trouble for having a private conversation with me," she said, "and your supervisor doesn't need to know anything about it."

Harper let out a sigh. "I don't know what you want me to tell you, anyway. I don't know who killed Kadeem. We hadn't even been dating that long."

"How long, exactly?"

"About four months. Since March, I think. We weren't serious, just out to have some fun, and I don't know everything that was going on in his life…"

"Tell me about the guy you were seeing before Kadeem. What's his name? Anthony? Antoine?"

Harper swung her head around like a startled deer. "Antoine Morrison? What does he have to do with this?"

"You were seen having a heated conversation with him this past weekend–and it wasn't the first time. Care to tell me about that?"

"Look, if it's any of your business, I've run into Antoine a few times at the club since we broke up. He's pushy and mouthy and jealous, and that's why I broke up with him in the first place. He'd been coming up to me and my friends, telling me I needed to drop Kadeem and get back together with him. I told him to leave me alone, but he doesn't seem to get the message. I don't need him telling me what I can and can't do, who I can and can't spend time with."

"I've been told he had a particular problem with

your dating an Arab-American."

"He has a problem with me being with anybody but him." Amirah watched her patiently, her eyebrows raised, and after a moment, the girl added, "But yes, he said some things about Kadeem. I wasn't going to let that bother me. No matter what he says, it's my life, and I'll live it however I want to."

"What exactly did he say?"

"I don't know. He just ran his mouth the way he always does. He said something about how I was going to be sorry for dating a towelhead, and how before long I'd be coming back to him because I'd see what a real man could do. The typical garbage he always says." Harper made a derisive sound. "He acts big like that, like he's some gangbanger, but he comes from the suburbs like the rest of us."

"What did you think he meant, you'd see what a real man could do?"

"Who knows? He's all hot air." The young woman's face went pale as the realization of what he might have been implying struck her. "At least, I thought he was just talking. You don't think–"

"Has he ever threatened you, or hurt you physically?"

"No–at least...I mean, he's never slapped me or hit me, anything like that."

The girl's comment made several questions pop into Amirah's head, but she only said, "So Antoine has a temper. Did he know where Kadeem lived?"

"I don't know...I mean, it wasn't a secret or anything, so he could've found out from my friends..."

"Could he have gotten hold of Kadeem's email address somehow? Not his personal one, but his work email?"

Harper stared at her. "I can't see how."

"Did Kadeem have a Facebook page, or something similar?"

"Yeah, we all do. I'm not on mine a lot, and neither was Kadeem, but I guess someone could've stalked him on it. You're sure Antoine had something to do with what happened to him?"

"There's only one way to be certain," Amirah said. "Do you have his phone number or his address?"

"Geez, I deleted his number from my phone a while ago. I can tell you where he lives, though."

Amirah carefully entered the address into her phone, as well as the last known place Antoine Morrison worked.

"It sounds as if Antoine isn't the only jealous person you know," she said when she finished. "What were you saying about your supervisor, that if he found out you were dating Kadeem, he wouldn't like it?"

Harper shrugged. "What can I say? Mr. Caffey gets so insecure when he sees me talking to guys my age. I don't tell him about who I'm dating. I don't need him to worry about me or anything."

Amirah looked at her and wondered where exactly her problem lay. Did the girl simply attract possessive men, or did she have trouble establishing clear boundaries when dealing with the male half of the species?

"Thank you, Miss Ashby. And don't worry, our conversation will be entirely confidential."

The young woman flashed her a sharp glance before she climbed out of the car, and as she nipped along the sidewalk, Amirah couldn't decide what bothered Harper Ashby more, her boyfriend being murdered or her being dragged into the investigation of his death.

Chapter 8

At about the time Amirah was pulling into the parking lot of Palladin Logistics, the final partner in Gates and Gates Investigations, Trick Nevill, was reclining behind the wheel of the oldest vehicle in the agency's fleet.

His given name was Patrick Nevill, but he had been known as "Trick" since he was a teenager, by his own insistence. He was on the other side of fifty, with dark eyes that slanted up slightly at the corners under thick eyebrows and longish, slightly wavy hair that was laced with gray. He looked like a biker more than anything else, an effect enhanced by the spotless black tank tops he favored, which fully displayed the tattoos across his biceps. As usual, he was carrying a handgun in a holster on his belt–not at the side, like most people would wear it, but in the small of his back. Mason Gates had commented more than once that it had to make sitting uncomfortable, but Trick always shrugged and said he'd gotten used to it being there.

The two men were not close friends, and had not been even when they were still on the force, but they had shared a yearning to move into the private sector and enough capital between them to collaborate in opening their own agency. Trick had quickly realized what Amirah Gates had learned in her turn: the typical cases a private agency handled were apt to be on the tedious side, and although the pay was better, it wasn't so by much of a margin. Lately, he had started taking outside jobs for various law firms, which Mason did not begrudge him in the least.

He was parked at the curb of a residential street in Greenmont, a neighborhood that sat firmly on the line between lower-class and lower-middle-class, in a twelve-year-old white Kia Rio with no hubcaps that was just shabby-looking enough to make it perfect for surveillance work.

Since surveillance by a private individual could be legally defined as stalking if the authorities were in the right mood, the sensible approach was to go about it as inconspicuously as possible. This ruled out parking directly in front of the subject's house like a paparazzo. Instead, he was positioned across the street and several doors down, behind a boxy gray Ford van, with his seat reclined as much as he could and still see through the driver's-side window—all of this meant to minimize his visual profile, should someone happen to glance in his direction.

The subject, in this case, was one Richard Daniel Reeves, age twenty-eight. He was unmarried, lived in a duplex apartment with his roommate, Amal Wright, and worked as a bagger at a nearby Elby's Foods. Approximately two and a half weeks earlier, Reeves had been in an automobile accident, rear-ended while pulling out of a gas station. Admittedly, the incident was the other driver's fault—he hadn't braked quite soon enough to avoid a collision—but the man swore up and down that he'd barely tapped the other car; that when he climbed out of his Subaru to exchange information, the only damage he'd seen on Reeves' vehicle were a few light scratches on the rear bumper.

Shortly afterward, Reeves' insurance company presented something more than the usual claim against the other driver. According to Reeves–and the accompanying doctor's report–he was in constant back, neck, and arm pain from the accident, to the point where he had had to take an indefinite amount of time off work and could not even hold a coffee cup for more than a minute or two. After a little digging, the second driver's insurer–Supreme Insurance, located in the same strip mall as Gates and Gates Investigations–found that Reeves had a history of these kinds of claims, and the office manager contacted Mason about proving this latest one a fraud.

That had been around the middle of the previous week. Since then Mason had gathered background information on Reeves and interviewed some of his coworkers at Elby's, and now Trick was on to the principal part of the investigation: following and watching the subject as he went about his usual routine, waiting to catch him on camera doing something that showed he was feigning his injuries.

To describe the work as unexciting would have been generous. The only things moving within sight were trees and bushes being stirred by a steady west wind. Trick had seen no sign of human activity all morning, and if it hadn't been for the semi-maintained look of the front yards, he could easily have believed the neighborhood was abandoned.

Finally, at about 2:50, the door of 1746B opened and the subject emerged. Reeves was a hefty young man with greasy black hair, wearing an oversized Arctic Monkeys T-shirt and denim cargo shorts. Trick lifted his phone above the edge of the window and brought its camera into focus, but Reeves behaved exactly as someone in his position would be expected to act. He walked slowly and stiffly down the porch steps and over to his car, eased open the door, and began the process of carefully and laboriously lowering himself into the driver's seat.

Which meant, Trick thought, that either he actually was injured from the accident, or he was savvy enough to know there was a good chance someone was watching him.

Reeves backed his car into the street and moved away unhurriedly in the opposite direction. Trick grabbed at the seat lever to spring himself upright and turned the key in the ignition, not bothering to fumble at the seat belt until he had swung out from the curb and had Reeves' maroon Nissan in sight at the far end of the block. The slight delay in his departure was not a bad thing. If he had started his engine the moment Reeves had started his, the sound would have been obvious in the quiet street and would have tipped the young man off that he was under observation.

Trailing a suspect is a balancing act: the pursuer has to stay close enough to the target vehicle to keep it in view and not be tripped up by changing traffic lights or other drivers, and yet far enough away to allow the subject to convince himself that he isn't being followed. Ideally, traffic surveillance involves two or more units in radio communication that can switch positions as circumstances dictate, but their agency was far too small for that sort of maneuver.

Thankfully, Trick had no problem following his subject. Reeves drove within the speed limit and yielded at every yellow light, and the dark red color of his car meant that visibility was not an issue.

It was not until they reached the end of the journey that trouble developed. Reeves' destination was Chaplet Center Mall, to the southeast. It was a smaller plaza, and like malls all across the country, had seen a downward trend in terms of sales and foot traffic, but on that afternoon, the parking lot was packed full of vehicles. Trick wondered if there was some sort of special event being held.

Reeves entered the parking lot and headed for the primary lane, the one lined up with the main entrance. Trick expected to have him creep around the lot for several minutes before he came to a stop, given the number of visitors, but surprisingly, Reeves found a parking spot almost at once, the only open space in that entire lane. Trick passed him and swung around into the next lane, under the assumption that he could find a space there and easily observe Reeves' actions.

It was not until he had driven down three more lanes that he found an empty space, and quickly realized he couldn't see Reeves' car from there. He sighed and climbed out of the Kia with his camera in hand.

He weaved between the parked cars and trucks, trying to find a position to see the subject without being noticed and without sticking out like a sore thumb.

He had just crossed one of the lanes, inching his way closer to Reeves' vehicle in a semi-crouch, when a small white pickup drew up behind him and a voice said, "Sir! Sir, step away from that vehicle."

Trick glanced back over his shoulder. The door that was swinging open on the truck bore a security company logo, and the driver climbing from the cab was clad in a tan uniform. Trick swore under his breath and turned to face the man.

He raised the hand holding the camera into the air and with his other hand reached slowly for the back pocket where he kept his wallet.

The security guard was a young man, pudgy and red-haired, and looked nervous. The Chaplet Center Mall had recently increased its security staff, with the shift away from department stores to flea markets and pawn shops, and he had only been on the job for two weeks.

He glimpsed the pistol at Trick's waist as he pulled up, and when the detective moved his hand in that direction, the guard reacted instantly. He whipped the canister of pepper spray from his belt, not being supplied with a gun, and pulled the trigger.

Unfortunately, the wind had changed by that point. No longer was it steadily blowing from the west, but it had turned gusty, and every few minutes shifted direction. The spray emerged from the nozzle in a thick stream and immediately blew back into the guard's face.

He turned scarlet and bent double, coughing and weeping, and that was when Trick made his next mistake.

He took a step toward the young man, saying, "Hey, buddy, you all right? Just breathe–"

The breeze shifted, and the cloud of irritant drifted to its original target, straight at him. Within seconds, both were hunched over, eyes and noses streaming, wheezing and retching.

Trick was the first to recover, but by the time he

could focus adequately enough to slip away and check on his subject, almost thirty minutes had passed and Richard Daniel Reeves was long gone.

Chapter 9

At a few minutes past six, for the second time that day, Mason headed down the ramp into the dim coolness of the Farquhar Building's parking garage.

This time, the attendant who had discovered Kadeem Nassar's body was on duty. Cayetano Robles was round in his torso and face, and the neatly-trimmed hair on his head was an even mixture of black and white. The nametag on his uniform, as his daytime counterpart had hinted, said CHUCK. When he spoke, it was with a very faint Mexican accent, indicating to Mason that he'd been living in the United States for many years.

Mason passed him his business card, and Robles considered it carefully, holding it with both hands.

"You working for the police?"

"No," Mason said. "Our agency is working for Mr. Nassar's family. I understand you were on duty when he was killed."

"That's right. I didn't see nothing, though."

From his tone, it sounded as if he had been beating himself up over the events of that Wednesday evening. Mason kept his expression sympathetic.

"Can you tell me what happened?"

The older man shook his head slightly. "I don't know if I should talk to you. You're working for his family; maybe they want to sue somebody…"

"No, Mr. Robles," Mason said quickly, "nobody is trying to get anyone in trouble. They don't think you're to blame, or that the Farquhar's management is to blame. They simply want to find out who killed Kadeem. Can you help us?"

Robles nodded. "It was about twenty minutes after I came on duty Wednesday. I walked the perimeter when I got here, same as I always do, and I never saw nothing suspicious… Then, about twenty minutes later, Mr. Perryman came running around the corner to the booth here, yelling his head off. That's Arnold Perryman, he's a retired pilot, lives on the seventh floor. Something's happened, he said, call 9-1-1. I followed him back to see what the trouble was, and I found Mr. Nassar lying on the ground next to his car. I checked for a pulse, but he didn't have any, even though he was still warm. It's funny, there was hardly any blood at all, but I heard afterward he was stabbed in the heart…"

Mason nodded as well. "It happens that way, sometimes. Did you see or hear anything out of the ordinary before this Mr. Perryman came to get you?"

Robles gave an aggrieved shake of his head. "No, nothing, nothing. The police had me and Mr. Redhoffer–that's the boss, the building superintendent–in his office after they took the body away, and they had us run through the security tapes. I guess the killer walked in through the lobby upstairs at about six-fifteen, and then came down the emergency stairs to the garage and headed for Mr. Nassar's car. He kept close to the outside wall, in the shadows, so he wouldn't be noticed. I would've had my back to him like this, facing the incoming cars, and I had no idea he was there. I guess I'm getting too old to do my job. I should've seen him…"

It's an odd but consistent part of human nature, when a tragedy occurs, to feel guilty about things that are entirely out of a person's control. Mason asked quietly, "Did the police get any idea of the killer's identity from the tapes?"

"No, not that I could tell. They got some pictures of him, but none of them real clear. This is an old building, and some of the cameras got put up in corners where they don't always get a good view. He was wearing one of those sweaters, a black sweater with a hood, you know, and he kept the hood over his head the whole time."

"But it was definitely a man on the tape?"

Robles shrugged. "I guess it was. The police thought it was."

They broke off their conversation as vehicles entered the garage, two luxury sedans in a row, and Robles had to park each of them. Mason thought it would have been quicker for the driver of the second car to park himself rather than wait for the attendant to finish with the first, but he supposed that was one of the perks the residents were paying for.

When the attendant returned, Mason said, "I've been told the killer took all the money from Kadeem's wallet."

"Yes, sir. Mr. Nassar's wallet was on the ground next to him, open, when I found him."

"And he scratched a message on the side of Kadeem's car."

Robles nodded. "That's what they told me. I didn't notice it myself. I was too busy trying to get hold of the police."

"What did you think when you heard about the message–'Die Arab'?"

The man shook his head sadly. "There's always people in this world who hate other people. Maybe it makes them feel better about themselves, I don't know. I heard plenty of those names myself over the years, ever since I came here from Coahuila. But I never thought something like this would happen here, in this building…"

"Did Kadeem ever say anything to you about getting threatened recently, or being worried about his safety?"

"He wouldn't talk to me about things like that. I'm just the old man who parks the cars, you know?"

"You haven't heard of any similar incidents in the building, of tenants being attacked or frightened?"

"No, no…"

There was nothing else Robles could tell him that was useful, and Mason thanked him for his time. When he emerged from the underground garage onto the sidewalk, a gunmetal-gray car was just pulling to a stop at the curb. It was clearly an unmarked police cruiser, and the man who climbed out, judging from his compact stature, black suit, and fedora, could only have been Detective Jensen.

He said sharply, in a tone meant to halt the other man in his tracks, "Gates!"

Mason stopped duteously. Jensen strode up to him, grabbed him by his upper arm, and hustled him into the passenger seat of the cruiser. He then marched around the car, seated himself behind the wheel, and launched into a speech.

"I thought it was you the minute I saw you coming out of that garage. I remember when you were with the DA's office, Gates, and I know all about how you quit the force to start your own agency. Well, I'm going to say this to you, and I'm going to say it only once—I don't care how successful you think you've gotten in the public sector, and I don't care who you're working for. I want you to stay out of my way. I don't need you interrogating my witnesses, poking around my crime scene, and interfering with my investigation. Do we understand each other?"

Mason listened politely, with raised eyebrows, and when the other man finished, he replied mildly, "Feeling better? Detective, I'm a private citizen, and the people working at the Farquhar Building are private citizens, and you know as well as I do, there's no law preventing two citizens from discussing whatever current events they like, even a recent murder. Unless you're planning on holding Mr. Robles as a material witness, which, based on what little he could tell me, doesn't seem likely."

He went on before Jensen could respond. "Look, why don't you let me buy you a cup of coffee? There's a coffeehouse about three blocks north of here. All I ask is that you get me back before my parking meter runs out."

It took a minute or two of internal debate, but eventually Jensen agreed, and before long, they were seated opposite each other at a round table with a pair of steaming lattes in front of them and a thick slice of cranberry orange loaf at the policeman's right hand.

Anyone who didn't know Arthur Jensen might have suspected that he wore stylish hats simply to hide his baldness, but he removed his fedora as soon as they sat down and set it carefully to one side without the least bit of self-consciousness. He took a sip of his coffee and nodded his approval.

"It makes a change from the watery brew they have back at the station house, at least. So…did you find out anything?"

Mason smiled. "To be frank, I didn't learn a single thing I hadn't already heard this morning when I interviewed the day-shift attendant. Detective, I want you to know that I don't think we're in competition here. We're both headed for the same goal. I'm working for Kadeem Nassar's family, and they want you to find his killer every bit as much as you do."

"Even more, I'm sure. But they think I'm on the wrong trail."

It wasn't a question, but a statement of fact. Mason spread his hands in a conciliatory gesture.

"The impression I've been given," he said, "is that you believe he was killed during a robbery attempt. His family is certain there's more to it than that, and they just want to make sure no possibilities get overlooked."

"Maybe so. But you were a cop long enough to know how it has to work. At a time like this, the family's emotions are running high, they're jumping to conclusions and grasping at every straw they can get their hands on. I can't let their feelings dictate the direction of the investigation. I don't have that luxury. I have to proceed based on the evidence, based on patterns of crime and criminal behavior, not based on some out-on-a-limb theory.

"Here are the facts as we have them. Kadeem Nassar's wallet was emptied of cash and credit cards by his killer. He was known by his friends and casual acquaintances to carry a good amount of money on him. On more than one occasion, he frequented a bar near his apartment called the Bottle Neck. Someone else who frequents the Bottle Neck regularly is a fellow by the name of Scotty Carryll."

Jensen reached into an inner pocket and drew out a black-and-white photograph of a man in his twenties, skinny and slightly wall-eyed, with dingy blond hair and a short goatee.

"Here he is. Looks like a real prize, doesn't he? Carryll has a long criminal record, including multiple counts of armed robbery, usually with something like an X-Acto knife. His father was a printer, and Carryll grew up around those kind of knives–the kind of knife, coincidentally, that the ME's office says was responsible for Nassar's death. Sounds like it's starting to fit together, doesn't it?

"That's my reason for stopping by the Farquhar Building this evening, to see if the parking attendant or anyone else saw someone fitting Carryll's description hanging around in the days leading up to the murder. This killing wasn't spur-of-the-moment. The killer had to've taken time to scope out the scene, had to've been aware that Nassar visited the gym on certain nights of the week in order to be waiting for him at that particular time."

"Does this Carryll have any kind of alibi for last night?"

"We don't know yet. No one's seen him since Wednesday evening. We have an APB out, though, and we'll lay our hands on him sooner or later."

"What do you make of the message scratched in

the side of the victim's car? Does your suspect have any history of hate crimes?"

Jensen stared levelly at him. "You ever shoot anyone, Gates?"

Mason blinked at the seemingly abrupt change of subject, and said slowly, "Yes, I fired my weapon in the line of duty."

"Then you know it's a lot easier to shoot someone, or attack someone when your blood is running high. That's what happened in that parking garage. You can count on it. The security tape shows Carryll ducked out of sight alongside Nassar's car when he got there, waiting for his target to show up. He's associated with racist groups in the past, even though he's never been convicted of a hate crime. So what did he do? He spent the time waiting, working himself up, thinking of all the ways life's kicked him in the teeth while this Middle Eastern kid is just rolling in money, giving himself the adrenaline boost he needed to commit an assault on someone he knows."

Mason nodded. "It's a theory. But there's something you don't know about Kadeem Nassar. Before he died, he was receiving death threats."

Jensen narrowed his eyes. "The family told you that?"

"More than that. His sister showed us the emails. Three of them, over the space of a month and a half, the last one the day before he died. We're combing over his laptop now to see if there's anything else to learn."

The policeman nodded thoughtfully. "Any indication who sent them?"

"Not yet."

"Okay. I'll need that laptop."

Mason took a sip of his coffee. "I'll get it to you as soon as I can."

Chapter 10

"As soon as you can?" echoed Amirah Gates. "Were you intending to take it to him tomorrow? Because I don't think Sa'id is finished with it yet."

They were sitting at a table in the middle of Ranger's, a casual dining restaurant not far from their office, with their secretary, Cecilia. Ranger's was a popular chain any day of the week, with its large buffet selection and flattop grill where the patrons could hand-pick a cut of steak and watch it being cooked, and on a Friday evening, it was packed wall-to-wall.

Mason grinned. "Until we hear otherwise, Sa'id can take as long as he needs with that laptop. I never promised a day or a time."

Cecilia, her eyes on the door, said, "There he is. Oh, he doesn't see me waving!"

They had a fourth place set at their table, awaiting the arrival of her boyfriend, Vaughn. She had, upon leaving work, let down her heavy blond hair so that it fell around her shoulders, minimizing the effect of her long neck. In Mason's opinion, it looked more attractive like that than the way she arranged it during office hours. He wondered if that was how she normally wore it, or if it was a special touch for her boyfriend's benefit.

Amirah glanced at him and tilted her head in the direction of the entrance. "Sweetheart?"

Mason pushed his chair back and threaded his way between the tables and through the crowd to the front of the building. Amirah gazed after him, and said, "Mmm. I'm glad he lets me pick out his clothes. It makes watching him walk away a lot more enjoyable."

Cecilia, wide-eyed, automatically glanced in the direction her boss was looking, and when she caught Amirah's glance, she blushed and quickly lowered her eyes to her plate. Amirah laughed impishly.

"Don't worry, I'm not the jealous type. You're allowed to agree with me that my husband has a nice physique. I just expect you not to spend all day at work checking him out. That might not be very productive," she added with a grin.

Mason returned with a second man in tow, slim and angular, with a mop of curly red hair and a bushy mustache. Cecilia rose halfway from her seat to kiss him on the corner of his jaw.

"Hiya, Vaughn. Sit here, Sweet Pea."

When they were all settled and Vaughn had placed his order, Amirah said, "So, where are we on the case?" She turned toward their guest. "That is, if you don't mind us talking shop in front of you?"

Vaughn smiled. "No, I don't mind. I'm pretty sure it's more interesting than the work stories I have–unless you really want to hear about penguin poop."

Vaughn was one of the keepers at the Tasker County Zoo, working primarily with the penguins and other birds in the Polar Circle exhibit.

"So," Amirah repeated, "where are we? We're sure Kadeem Nassar wasn't killed by a mugger?"

"We're sure," Mason said.

She slanted her large hazel eyes up at her husband.

"Okay, we're sure, but would you mind telling us all why that is? The official theory, Detective Jensen's theory, is that he was killed in a robbery."

He shook his head. "Jensen is a sharp dresser, but he isn't a sharp thinker. His idea is that their suspect, a habitual armed robber with racist tendencies, needed to work himself up to a killing pitch while he was waiting for Kadeem to arrive, and that's why he scratched that message in the side of the car. They should've known, as soon as they saw the message, that robbery wasn't the motive…

"There are only two possibilities: either the killer etched the message beforehand while waiting for his victim to arrive, or he left it afterward, before fleeing the scene. No matter which of those we pick, we're left with the same conclusion. No robber, assuming his motive is solely monetary, is going to hang around the scene of his crime, increasing his chances of being identified or caught, just to leave behind some hate manifesto. And if the killer took the time to cut that message into the side of the car first, before Kadeem was attacked, it would indicate he'd already made up his mind to commit the murder."

"The killer couldn't have been trying to draw attention away from the robbery by leaving that message, could he?" asked Cecilia.

"Or," said Vaughn, wanting to keep up his end of the conversation, "what if the killer and the person who left the message were two different people?"

Cecilia stared at her boyfriend, startled. Mason, wanting to treat the other man's suggestion fairly, prodded at his salad before answering.

"It's possible the two things aren't related, but the

odds against it are pretty high. We'd have to believe that either two different strangers were present in that parking garage around the time Kadeem was killed–which is something no one's made any mention of so far, including the police, and no other suspicious individuals seem to have shown up on the security tapes–or that the message on the car was left a good deal earlier than the murder. We know Kadeem didn't tell anyone about the threatening emails he was getting, but it's hard to imagine a racially-charged warning like that being on the side of his car for any length of time without someone noticing.

"As to the other point, if the killer was trying to distract attention from the robbery by scratching that message on the car, why go and leave the open wallet in plain sight beside the body?" Mason shrugged. "As a crime scene, it doesn't make a lot of sense. I'm beginning to suspect the killer of providing too many motives for his crime."

"To sum up, then," said Amirah, "we don't know why Kadeem Nassar was killed, other than it probably wasn't to rob him. On the other hand, we do know the killer has to be familiar with Kadeem's schedule, to know he'd be in the parking garage around six-thirty last night. And thanks to Sa'id, that's not all we know."

She told them the latest information her cousin had gathered from the victim's laptop. "He was able to trace which server the three threatening emails originated from. Well, not the exact server, but at least the general location of it. It came from a server in Canfield Tower, the home of CanCorp, where Kadeem just happens to have been working as an auditor for the last two months."

Mason raised his eyebrows, and Vaughn whistled softly.

"You're talking about the Canfield Corporation?" he asked. "That massive brokerage firm downtown?"

Amirah nodded.

"Wow. You guys are swinging in the big leagues now…"

"It at least narrows the suspect pool," Mason murmured.

"Only if the emails really are connected with his murder," Amirah added. "It's crossed my mind they may not be. There's nothing so far that definitely proves they are, even though Leila Nassar is convinced they are, and the messages themselves don't give any clue one way or the other."

Mason nodded. "You're right. Coincidences do happen, but I've learned to be leery of them when it comes to murder cases. For now, let's proceed under the assumption the two are connected, at least until we come up against some evidence that proves the opposite."

"Speaking of the corporation," Cecilia said, "you have an appointment with them tomorrow."

Mason glanced from her to his wife questioningly.

"Oh, yes," Amirah said. "Cecilia got a call from CanCorp this afternoon, asking us to meet with a representative of their company regarding Kadeem Nassar's death. Ten a.m. at the Pietermaritz Plaza. What do you think of that, husband of mine?"

Her husband popped a forkful of his beef Stroganoff into his mouth without replying and chewed slowly and thoughtfully.

Chapter 11

The Pietermaritz Plaza Hotel was a blocky eggshell-colored building that took up an entire block on the north side of the city, so that it was either two streets south of the river or one, depending on whether a person was counting from the main entrance or the service dock. Not surprisingly, for a Saturday morning, the surrounding streets were mostly empty.

Mason and Amirah Gates entered the hotel's east entrance, which led directly to the conference rooms, and at first, there was no one at all in sight, just a long stretch of hallway covered in patterned crimson carpet.

She told her husband, "Conference Room C, they said."

When they stepped around the corner and neared the room, a man standing beside the door stepped forward to intercept them.

"Gates and Gates? You're on time. I'll need to search you before I can let you inside. You don't have a problem with that, I hope?"

Amirah's eyes widened. The man was tall and broad, with the massive frame of a former football player stretching his tan sharkskin suit tight across his biceps and thighs. His buff-colored hair, though full on top, tapered to an almost military cut on the sides. His thick fingers moved over them with professional exactness. Amirah surrendered the pepper spray canister she habitually carried in her purse, and Mason gave up his pocketknife, and these went into the man's hip pocket.

He held the conference room door open for them to enter and then followed them in.

There were two people seated at the table inside. The first was a stocky woman with her dark hair cut medium-short and a large topaz-and-onyx giraffe pinned to the lapel of her charcoal blazer. The second individual was a man in his mid-sixties with a squarish face, silvery hair, and keen black eyes. As he rose to shake their hands, Mason noted that his three-piece suit, though cut conservatively, was more expensive than it seemed at first glance, and solid silver cuff links gleamed at the ends of his sleeves. As soon as he introduced himself, the need for a bodyguard during their visit became obvious.

"Jerald Hartwell Canfield IV. I don't suppose I need to explain who I am to you."

"You're the president of CanCorp. Mason Gates. My wife Amirah."

"President, and chairman of the board of directors, and so on. In view of the situation that's arisen within the company, I thought it would be best for me to be a part of this conference. This is Janeen Walkowitz, our Director of Accounting. Please, have a seat. Janeen will walk you through the general picture. You can proceed, Janeen."

The woman cleared her throat and adjusted her blazer before starting. "I received a phone call from Terrence Plant, the head of Certified Accounting Associates, yesterday afternoon in regards to Kadeem Nassar. We had been contracting CAA–Mr. Nassar specifically–to assist in an internal audit at CanCorp, and based on his conversation with someone from your agency, Mr. Plant had concerns that he wanted to pass on to me. After discussing those concerns, we felt it would be best to reach out to you about the situation we're dealing with.

"Our internal audit began a little over a month and a half ago. Mr. Plant informs me that around that same time, Mr. Nassar began receiving threats–something we were unaware of until now. We were under the impression his death was simply an unfortunate, random incident. If the threats he received really do have some connection with his death, and if they have anything at all to do with our company, then we want to extend our full cooperation to you in finding the source of those threats."

The two detectives waited, but the woman folded her hands in front of her and said nothing further. Mason frowned in disbelief.

"With all due respect, there's more to it than that, isn't there? As busy as someone like you is, Mr. Canfield, you wouldn't have gone to the trouble of arranging this meeting just to tell us something that could've been conveyed over the telephone. Just what is this situation in your company that made it so important for you to sit in this morning?

"I'm going to take a leap and guess it's related to a question we've been wondering: Why would a multibillion-dollar company the size of yours need to hire an outside firm to help perform an internal audit?"

Neither of them responded immediately, and Mason added, "It may interest you to know, our tech expert has determined that those threatening emails

Kadeem Nassar received definitely originated from one of your company's servers. Now that could mean one or two things, but…"

The two executives exchanged glances. The bodyguard, standing against the wall with his arms crossed over his chest, had no expression at all on his face.

Canfield appeared to come to a decision. He cleared his throat and leaned forward, clasping his hands together on the dull laminate surface of the conference table.

"Like any publicly listed corporation," he said, "an audit board monitors our internal procedures. In our case, the audit board is composed of three outside directors and two inside directors, one of whom is Ms. Walkowitz. Approximately two months ago, she brought to my attention a discrepancy the board had uncovered. In a very short time, it became apparent that it was not a mistake in our bookkeeping, but a deliberate embezzlement involving thousands of accounts. As far as we can determine, the theft was not the result of an outside operator hacking our mainframe; in that case, they would have taken as much as they could in as short a time as possible. What we've uncovered instead appears to be a systematic siphoning of small amounts over a prolonged period, engineered by someone inside CanCorp.

"Ordinarily, the next step would be an internal audit, carried out by Accounting, to track the theft to its source, but in this case, it seemed more prudent to use an independent auditor, someone with no obvious affiliation with the company.

"At the same time, though I don't intend to bore

you with the details, there has been dissatisfaction on the board, and indications are that certain directors are maneuvering to have me replaced. A fraud of this scope, once it becomes public knowledge, will only provide further fuel for a coup. What I would like, ideally, would be to determine who is responsible for the theft and get the monies returned to our clients' accounts before the rest of the board can discover what's happened, thereby reducing the opposition's leverage and increasing mine. It occurred to us that your agency may be able to assist us in finding the person responsible."

It was Mason and Amirah's turn to look at one another. Fortunately, they were *simpatico* in most things, including this one, and there was no need for them to discuss their response.

Mason said, "I'm not sure how much we could do for you. We're not an accounting firm. I imagine you'll have someone continue the auditing work Kadeem was doing–possibly someone else from his company?"

"That seems to be our best strategy at this point," Ms. Walkowitz said.

"We may be able to do some investigating for you, if any indications come to light as to the person responsible, but if we were to take you on as a client I'd be concerned about a potential conflict of interest."

"How so?" asked Canfield.

"We're working for Leila Nassar first and foremost. Her sole instructions are for us to find the person who killed her brother. Your primary concern is to recover the stolen funds, whether that leads to an arrest or not. I take it from what you've said so far that no one outside the company has any idea the money is missing?"

"No. The amounts being taken from the individual accounts, in themselves, are quite small, small enough to appear to be bookkeeping errors at first glance."

"You can see our dilemma, then. We want to do the best we can for our initial client, which could well include making the authorities aware of the embezzlement. You, on the other hand, would rightly expect us to put your interests first, and keep the matter under wraps as much as possible." Mason held up his hand before the other man could interrupt. "I have a suggestion that may help both of us. We could send someone into your company undercover, to try to ferret out Kadeem Nassar's killer from the inside. If the killing turns out to have nothing to do with the embezzlement, we'll be free to continue investigating for you, without any conflict. If the two are connected, maybe you can work out some arrangement with the district attorney's office before an arrest is made, to retrieve the stolen funds and protect your company's reputation."

"I see. You already have an operative in mind?"

"Yes," Amirah said. "Me. I'll do it."

Maybe they weren't as *simpatico* as Mason thought. He flicked his eyes toward his wife in the briefest of glances. They hadn't discussed this possibility beforehand, since the scheme had only just then occurred to him, and in fact, he had intended to ask Trick Nevill to take on the assignment, but from the decisive way she'd answered he knew the matter was as good as settled.

"That's our proposal," he said blandly. "When do we start?"

Chapter 12

Mason sighed and shifted slightly in the driver's seat of the Kia Rio.

Despite his confident demeanor in front of the CanCorp executives that morning, he was worried. He appreciated his wife's enthusiasm. It was one of the things he loved about her, but he was concerned that she was getting in over her head. She had only been working with him in the agency for a year, and in his opinion, that was hardly enough experience to plunge into an undercover hunt for a lethal criminal. What if the person they were looking for got an inkling of who she really was and cornered her? If that happened, there was nothing Mason could do about it until it was too late.

And, he had to admit, there was also nothing he could do to change her mind about going ahead.

It wasn't as if he could claim it was an unimportant avenue of investigation, one that she could leave to someone else. The circumstances of the murder made him certain the police department's suspect, the X-Acto-knife-wielding mugger, was a dead end. The ex-boyfriend of Kadeem Nassar's latest squeeze had made a better suspect, but they had stopped at his home after their interview at the Pietermaritz, and his grandmother had patiently explained that Antoine Morrison had been sitting at the dinner table, in full view of multiple family members, when Kadeem was killed. It was possible she was lying, but Mason highly doubted it.

He would have liked to think about something else, but the present circumstances were not helping. It was his turn at the Supreme Insurance surveillance job, and he was parked where Trick had been the day before, behind the broken-down gray Ford van on Bayberry Street in Greenmont. He had the two front windows rolled down and a telephoto lens propped on the driver's side windowsill, but apart from a faint breeze riffling the shrubbery and a bird or two warbling away in the shade, nothing was moving in the street. There were no signs of life at 1746B, although as far as he knew, both occupants were home. There was nothing at all to keep his mind from circling back around to his apprehensions about Amirah, like a dog nipping at a ragged ball from every side.

He was lost in thought when the handle of the passenger door clicked open. Startled, he jerked his head to the right to see his partner slip into the opposite seat and pull the door quietly shut behind him.

Trick made a face at him. "Don't get your panties in a bunch. It's only me. I parked around the corner, and they couldn't see me approaching the car with that van blocking their view. Anything yet?"

Like the other man, Mason kept his voice low, knowing that sound would carry in the stillness of the street.

"Not a thing."

"Well, that'll be changing shortly," Trick said in a satisfied tone. "I stopped at a courier service on my way over here and had them put together a little package our friend over there won't be able to refuse. A couple of phone books and two handfuls of copy paper, with a 1-Up label pasted on it. A tiny bit heavier than a coffee cup."

"Is that right?"

"Maybe it's a bit of a long shot, but I'm wagering if Reeves opens his door and sees a package labeled '1-Up… Grand Prize Inside' he isn't going to think twice about bending over and picking it up–and then we'll have him."

1-Up was the name of a local video arcade, which was regularly frequented by both Richard Daniel Reeves and his roommate. The detectives had learned during their background work on the case the two men were hardcore gamers, and this was Trick's idea of a sure-fire trap for the subject.

Mason showed no immediate reaction to the plan, and Trick, nettled by the lack of response, asked sourly, "Mind on other things, isn't it? Thinking about your wife?"

"Yes," Mason said and gave him a brief rundown on the outcome of their meeting with the CanCorp representatives. "She's never done any undercover work, and she's going to be pretty much on her own when she's there…"

Trick waited for a moment before responding. "You're not going to want me to say this, but it seems to me you crossed this bridge a long time ago, when you let her talk you into joining this agency. It was only a matter of time before she had to handle an assignment on her own. You didn't think she'd let you babysit her forever, did you? Besides, I know she's not exactly helpless."

"No," Mason echoed, "she's not helpless."

"But you're worried she's going to get into a situation she can't cope with?" Trick asked. "If you want, I can give her a few pointers before Monday. She is certified with a gun, isn't she?"

The other man shook his head briefly.

Although Mason, like Trick, had a firearms license, he rarely carried his handgun with him, and he had resisted suggesting to Amirah that she learn how to use one. In his experience as a cop, the presence of a gun could just as easily escalate a situation as defuse it. Not to mention that it would be awkward, if not impossible, for her to carry a pistol into a public place like Canfield Tower.

On the other hand, they periodically visited a local *dojang* for a self-defense refresher course, and he insisted she keep her pepper spray within reach. If he was being fair, Trick was right–she was levelheaded, and she could take of herself. But, he was still her husband, and he was going to be concerned about her.

About half an hour later, a young man with a goatee and a yellow-and-tan uniform trotted up the walk to 1746B, with a package under his arm. Per Trick's instructions, he deposited the box on the doormat, gave the doorbell a good firm ring, and departed posthaste.

The door opened. Reeves appeared in the doorway, his torso draped in a Cage the Elephants T-shirt this time, and glanced around. He spotted the box, and the label on it, immediately, but instead of reaching for it, he turned and called over his shoulder to his roommate. The answer he got back, whatever it was, evidently did not reassure him.

"He's moving the box," Mason whispered to his

partner, who could not see the front door from his side of the car.

"Great! So you're getting–"

"Not the way you think."

Reeves took one full step out onto his welcome mat (which read "Get Lost"), took another long glance around, and with the side of his foot, began to push the package slowly away from him. The house was divided into two apartments, and though each had its own front walk and steps, there was a shared concrete porch connecting them. Reeves, moving with the sort of care an injured man would be expected to show, nudged the box across the porch until it was resting in front of the other residence, and then, with his arm fully extended so that he was out of the direct line of sight, he rang the doorbell and retreated into his own apartment.

Mason described the suspect's activity tersely for his partner's benefit. Trick stared at him disbelievingly.

"Are you effing kidding me?"

Ten minutes went by, and then fifteen. There was no sign of activity from within 1746A. The door to 1746B was still cracked open; evidently, Reeves or his roommate were waiting for further developments.

"Nothing?" Trick asked.

Mason shrugged. "It doesn't look like today's our day. He's a veteran at this, and he's not going to give himself away on his own porch."

Trick shook his head and muttered under his breath, and then abruptly shoved his door open and pushed himself out of the car. Mason had no idea what he intended to do, and could only watch, his hand on his camera, in case it ended up producing the evidence they were after.

Trick headed up the walk of 1746A and reached the door without any sound or movement to indicate there was anyone on the other side. He mounted the porch and bent down to pick up the package.

At the very last moment, there must have been some faint noise from inside the apartment, because he lifted his head just as the inner door swung open and the storm door flew outward, banging him square on the nose.

He scuttled backward, still hunched over, clutching his nose. A small, spare woman in her fifties stood there, clad in a bathrobe and pajamas in the middle of the afternoon and waving a small broom in one hand.

"Just what do you think you're doing?" she demanded.

Trick straightened up. "Lady–"

She didn't pause for a second.

"Hoodlums, that's all you are!" she cried. "Going around stealing other folks' stuff!" She swatted him full in the face with the flat side of the broom.

Mason scrambled from his car and raced across the street. Trick's right foot slid off the edge of the porch and he fell hard on the concrete, clutching at the metal banister behind him. The woman continued to batter him with the broom while Trick swore fluently.

"I'll take it from here, ma'am," Mason said, flashing his PI license at her and doing his best Joe Friday impersonation. He slid his hand under his partner's left arm and hefted him to his feet. "We've had our eye on this one for some time."

They beat a hasty retreat while she glared at them, her fists planted on her hips.

"I think," Mason said when they reached Trick's

car around the corner, trying his best not to laugh, "we've done all the surveillance work we can this morning."

Trick was too disgusted to respond in more than single syllables.

Chapter 13

Canfield Tower rose from the heart of the business district like a tool shaped for giants, all planes and angles, gleaming silver and blue against the cloudless Monday morning sky.

At three minutes to seven, Amirah Gates crossed the street from the employee parking garage and entered one of the building's multiple front doors to find herself in a cavernous lobby. Empty space stretched above her head for half a dozen floors, and the clicking of her 3-inch heels against the polished tiles was quickly lost among the echoes from all the other foot traffic.

As instructed, she headed for the circular desk in the center of the lobby, behind which sat a guard in a white-and-brown uniform.

"Imani Bukhari, reporting for my first day at CanCorp," she said.

When she and Mason were discussing what name she would use while undercover, Amirah had suggested simply going by her middle name and maiden name. Mason had countered with an alternate suggestion: that she borrow the name of a certain one of her cousins. The advantage to that was that if the killer became suspicious and tried to check up on her, the trail would lead back to a real person–albeit one who happened to be vacationing in Corpus Christi that summer.

The guard glanced briefly at the clipboard in front of him and nodded. He handed her a plastic visitor's badge with an alligator clip and went into his spiel:

"...Must be worn at all times. Any guns, knives, or chemical sprays that could be used as a weapon must be surrendered and will be held in a lockbox here until claimed. Any photography or taking of video is prohibited unless authorized by approved company representatives. Do you have any questions?"

She left her pepper spray in the bottom of her purse, signed where indicated, and headed for the elevators. As the clear glass cage rose into the air, she was beginning to feel a little self-conscious. To dress for her role as a temp at the brokerage firm, she had picked out what she had thought was a simple outfit: a sleeveless white blouse with the top button unfastened, a plain black skirt, and a pair of black pumps. She had pulled her hair back in a loose ponytail to complete the look, hoping it would make her seem younger.

Judging from her husband's reaction, though, maybe she should have dressed more severely. He had propped himself up in bed on one elbow and whistled appreciatively, following that up with a humorous purr–and then flipped over and went back to sleep, since he didn't have to get up for another hour or so. She had rolled her eyes at him and gone to finish getting ready.

She glanced surreptitiously at the other occupants of the elevator. It was true that her skirt ended two inches above her knees, showing off more of her legs than she usually displayed in public, but her outfit was more or less interchangeable with what the other women were wearing. The problem was that with her figure, what looked neatly attractive on other women tended to make her look lushly inviting.

Amirah sighed. Someday she would be comfortable with her body. She just hoped it wouldn't take hitting menopause to do it.

Janeen Walkowitz was waiting for her in front of the reception desk on the forty-first floor, wearing a ballerina in pink garnet on her lapel. She shook Amirah's hand.

"Nice to meet you...Imani. This way."

They turned right down the corridor, into a large space filled with sets of cubicles, and continued down the left-hand side of the room, entering Ms. Walkowitz's office. Aside from the expected business furniture, a folding chair and square table had been squeezed into one corner. Amirah thought they had been placed there for her, but realized she was looking at the late Kadeem Nassar's work area.

Ms. Walkowitz closed the door behind them and waved Amirah into a chair in front of her desk.

The accounting head's desk was the tidiest Amirah had ever seen, particularly for someone in charge of the finances of an entire corporation. The few people she had met who did bookkeeping for a living tended to exist in a controlled avalanche of receipts, invoices, and ledgers, with pieces of paper threatening to drift everywhere. Here, every single form and sheet was confined to crisp-edged stacks, the pens and pencils in tidy alignment, and even the computer tower was spotless.

Ms. Walkowitz sat behind her desk and clasped her hands together.

"I've had HR enter you into our system as a floating temp, which will allow us to move you from department to department as needed during your investigation. In the meantime, we have no choice but to start over again with the internal audit. CAA is sending over another of their accountants this morning, and I'll have to bring him or her up to speed all over again."

"Tell me about the embezzlement," Amirah said, "keeping in mind that I only know the basics of bookkeeping."

The other woman took a deep breath. "Our firm handles thousands upon thousands of customer accounts every day, offering services that range from financial planning to retirement portfolios to stock trading. About two months ago, we discovered a series of small discrepancies in multiple accounts, where the totals of the amounts deposited in a given month did not match the end-of-month balance sheets. The discrepancy, in each case, was ten cents per account, once or twice a month. It was practically a fluke that we discovered it, and it's the sort of small amount that could easily have been a bookkeeping error, which is no doubt what the person responsible was counting on. If one or two of our customers complained, at the end of a year, they'd be out two dollars and forty cents at most, and we'd certainly be willing to recoup that small of an amount to them. All those cents will eventually add up, though. Let's say, as an example–" She reached for the adding machine on her desk. "—there are fifty thousand accounts involved. At the end of a year…our thief would have pilfered a hundred and twenty thousand dollars. Not exactly the heist of the century. But at the end of twenty years, the thief would have almost two and a half million dollars tucked away. It might not pay for an escape to the Cayman Islands, but it would make for a comfortable early retirement to the Florida Keys or the California coast."

"How can you be sure it isn't just a computer glitch causing the discrepancies?"

"Oh, that was the first thing we considered. We had our IT people scan the servers for programming errors, spyware, worms–anything you can think of, we looked for. They came up empty-handed. That money is being pulled into an account somewhere, but we don't have the faintest idea where. As Mr. Canfield told you, we're left with only one explanation–that someone inside the company is deliberately siphoning off funds into their own pockets."

She carefully replaced the adding machine in the exact position it had been in before.

"There's one other thing that tells us it isn't some kind of software issue. We have customers from Cheyenne to St. Louis, and beyond. As you can appreciate, our customers range from large companies to small families and individuals, from accounts with balances in the hundreds of thousands of dollars to accounts with only a few hundred dollars in them. In every case, this discrepancy has affected accounts above one thousand dollars, where theoretically, a missing ten or twenty cents a month wouldn't be as likely to be noticed. Not a single account with a balance below nine hundred ninety-nine dollars has been touched, as far as we can tell."

"So the thief is trying to be as discreet as possible. Did Kadeem mention any breakthroughs in the audit?"

"Not to me."

"Do you remember him interacting with anyone in

particular, or expressing any interest in a particular employee?"

"No, not that I recall. He met some of our accounting department when he started, but he purposely worked apart from them, since we so far have no way of knowing who can be trusted. As far as his dealings with employees outside of Accounting, I really couldn't say, but I can't imagine he had much to do with anyone here."

"How many people inside the company know about the work he was doing?"

Ms. Walkowitz sighed. "Very few, I hope. We were more than clear with his employer about the need to keep the details of his work strictly confidential, and it seemed to me Mr. Nassar understood that. The divisional managers in this department are aware of what's going on–that was unavoidable–but they're under strict instructions not to share information regarding the audit with their teams."

Amirah asked about the general organization of the accounting department.

"The company is organized into divisions by geographic region. We have four divisions: north, west, southeast, and southwest. Regional managers head each of those and oversee a team of three to four accountants, depending on the workload. Aside from Operations, that is, processing all of our clients' bills and statements, we also deal with payroll and insurance needs for all the corporation's employees. There's more than enough work to keep us busy, believe me. Even in this so-called digital age, you couldn't imagine the amount of paperwork a company this size generates in a month."

Ms. Walkowitz took her on a quick tour of the department, and introduced her to the four regional managers as a new hire. Some of them were friendly, others were more businesslike, but as she had said, they were all obviously quite busy.

Later in the morning, the replacement auditor from CAA arrived–the man called George, whom she had met before. He entered the accounting head's office with his unusual hitching step, no doubt the result of some old injury, wearing a tweed jacket with elbow patches and carrying a narrow, worn briefcase. He recognized her when he saw her, but he was sharp enough not to let it show in his face, which she appreciated.

At about ten o'clock she took a break and headed down the hallway to the break room in search of chocolate. The room was unoccupied when she entered except for a slim, black girl with her head bent over her phone. She glanced up from her table as Amirah passed, but before Amirah could say hello, her own phone buzzed.

It was her sister Aziza, with her latest brainwave for their parents' anniversary party: an extravagant cake.

"There's a new, Neo-French restaurant and bakery downtown called Parlenez. Have you and Mason been there yet? They make the most elegant cakes, and of course they'll decorate them for any occasion. I thought about getting them a heart-shaped cake first, with three tiers, and red fondant ribbons–so beautiful–but then I saw one that was iced in gold and silver, and that would be even classier, don't you think?"

Amirah sighed. "Aziza, you know how

conservative *baba* is. He isn't going to appreciate anything that screams 'Western decadence.' "

"What on earth are you talking about? How can he possibly object to a scrumptious cake?"

"Zee, please, just try and think traditional."

When her sister finally ended the call, Amirah sighed again and turned her attention to the vending machines. One of them had Oh Henry! Bars, which immediately boosted her spirits, and when she straightened up from the machine with her prize, the other girl was smiling at her.

"Hi. You must be new. My name's Nichele Bell, but everybody calls me Niki."

"Imani Bukhari."

"Bukhari? Like the restaurant chain–Bukhari's Family Dining? Are you related to them?"

"Something like that. It doesn't get me any free meals, though."

Niki laughed. Amirah came back to sit across from her. Niki had her own distinctive style: her wavy hair was pulled back in a pretty half-up afro, her blouse had a bold pattern in scarlet paisley, and her bright red flats were topped with rainbow-striped bows.

"So, what department are you in?" the girl asked, setting her phone down.

"Accounting."

"I'm in Marketing. We take up the other half of this floor. Accounting, huh? So–" She dropped her voice. "Are you taking over for that guy who was killed?"

"Killed?"

Amirah did her best to act clueless, but inwardly she was excited. She had been wondering how to subtly pump her new acquaintance for information, and here Niki was bringing up the subject without any prompting.

"They didn't tell you? It was all over the news this weekend, and everybody in Marketing's been talking about it this morning. Maybe they didn't want to scare you off on your first day…"

"Was he killed here? In the building?"

"Oh, no. Nothing like that. He was the victim of a hate crime, attacked in the parking garage of his high-rise. No, there's never been any trouble here at Canfield Tower, at least not in the three years I've been here."

"But he worked in Accounting?"

"Yeah, he'd been here about two—no, three months. His name was Kadeem."

"Did you know him well?"

"No, not really. I talked to him occasionally, but he didn't say a lot. He seemed sort of reserved. I mean, he was cute in a way, if you're into that kind, but—" Niki stopped in wide-eyed embarrassment. "Er, sorry, no offense."

It was Amirah's turn to laugh. "No, I know what you mean. We all have a type, don't we? What about him? Did he have a type?"

"You got me. I never saw him pay more than the usual attention to anyone here."

"And you don't think what happened to him had anything to do with his working at CanCorp?"

"I'd be surprised if it did… Although, just between you and me, there was an incident a while back, and it involved one of the bosses. I didn't see it myself, but apparently Kadeem got into an argument with the assistant vice-president of our marketing department.

They said Mr. Brisbane came close to decking him."

"You didn't hear what the argument was about?"

"No, but... well, Mr. Brisbane's pretty conservative. The way I've heard it, he's against women in the workforce, blacks and minorities in the workforce, you name it. Way old-school. It could be Mr. Brisbane just didn't like seeing him in the building."

"I'll have to watch out for this Brisbane, then."

"Yeah, I wouldn't make eye contact if you pass him in the hallways. Probably safer that way."

Amirah grinned. "I'll keep that in mind."

Chapter 14

At noon, Amirah found herself holding a plastic tray in her hands, staring up at a menu board listing such items as "Congo Crush" and "Peccary Panini." There was a rainforest-themed café on the west side of the ground floor of Canfield Tower, complete with fake palm trees and servers in safari hats, and a good percentage of CanCorp employees frequented it at lunchtime–mostly due to convenience' sake, she assumed, since the prices and selection didn't seem any better than those of other restaurants.

She worked her way through the line and came away with a chicken salad sandwich, sweet potato fries, and an orange cream soda, and headed toward the tables. As she passed the ones that looked out on the lobby, she stopped abruptly and said, "Oh, hello! Didn't I see you upstairs?"

She held her breath and hoped the question seemed spur-of-the-moment. The woman sitting alone at the table lifted her head and regarded her with a less than inviting expression. She was somewhere in her forties, with sandy brown hair pulled back in a single loose braid, and she was dressed austerely, in a plain white blouse and beige skirt suit. She was Frederick Brisbane Jr.'s secretary, and bore the unlikely name of Jan Butters.

"You work at CanCorp too?"

"I just started in the accounting department this morning. Do you mind?" Amirah plopped down across from her without waiting for an answer and dipped a couple of fries in the accompanying maple aioli sauce. "Of course, I'm just a temp, so I'm sure they'll put me wherever they want me. What department are you in?"

"Marketing."

"How's the work there? Any openings?"

"I couldn't say," Ms. Butters responded coolly. "I'm the private secretary to the Assistant Vice-President, and I'm not planning on vacating my position any time soon."

"How is he to work for?"

Ms. Butters paused slightly. "Mr. Brisbane is very good at what he does."

It was not really an answer to the question, but Amirah went on as though she hadn't noticed. She took a sizable bite of her chicken salad sandwich and chewed slowly.

"Probably been in marketing for years and years, I'll bet."

"As a matter of fact, Mr. Brisbane originally went into medical school. His father is a cardiothoracic surgeon at Community Medical-Midlands. He was there for two years before he changed fields and started here at CanCorp."

"Really? What made him decide to switch careers?"

"The work schedule was simply unmanageable. The kind of hours they expect from new doctors–and nurses, too, for that matter–it's absurd. Mr. Brisbane chose a field where he could work at a more reasonable pace."

Amirah took a sip of her soda and said, as though it had just struck her, "Brisbane? Your boss is Mr. Brisbane? I heard an independent contractor who used to work in my department got into an argument with a Mr. Brisbane a couple of weeks ago. You don't think it's the same person, do you?"

"Seeing that there's only one Brisbane at CanCorp," Ms. Butters said frostily, "I imagine it would have to be."

Amirah leaned in and asked, in a confidential tone, "Do you know what they argued about?"

The woman appeared doubtful about responding to the question, but it's an axiom of investigative work that given the opportunity and a little prompting, most people will willingly expound at length on their side of a given situation. Ms. Butters was no exception.

"I don't suppose there's any harm in telling you. After all, Mr. Brisbane has nothing to be ashamed of. Anyone would have responded the way he did. This contractor you're talking about–his name was Kareem, or something like that–insulted him in front of an elevator full of people. He claimed Mr. Brisbane made inappropriate advances toward another employee, a young woman on our floor. Of course, Mr. Brisbane responded strongly to those allegations. You wouldn't expect him to keep silent under the circumstances. Well, one thing led to another, and this Kareem ended up shoving Mr. Brisbane."

"They fought? Right there in the elevator?"

Ms. Butters frowned. "Hardly that…"

"But your boss put him in his place, didn't he?" On a hunch, Amirah added, "Probably told him he was lucky to even have a job here."

"Exactly! Now, I don't want you to get the wrong impression. Mr. Brisbane doesn't have a racist bone in his body. But he does have strong opinions about those people coming here and making trouble, acting as if everyone owes them something just because they've managed to make it to this country... That doesn't apply to you, of course–anyone can tell you were born here."

It was on the tip of Amirah's tongue to point out that Kadeem Nassar too had been a US citizen, born in a Cathedral City hospital like thousands of other people, but she held her peace. Ms. Butters, at any rate, swept on before she had a chance to say anything.

"Besides, his accusations were ridiculous, absolutely ridiculous. Mr. Brisbane happens to be engaged to Evangeline de Reis. Miss de Reis is a lovely young woman whose family has been in banking in this city for over a century. He certainly has no need to go chasing around after office temps!"

Amirah took a sip of her drink and nodded. "I'm sure you're right. It was probably just a lot of hot air over nothing. Isn't it funny how rumors get started, and things get blown all out of proportion? Actually, it's what happened after their argument that has everyone in Accounting talking."

The other woman narrowed her eyes. "What do you mean?"

"Haven't you heard? It was on the news over the weekend, that's why everyone is talking about it this morning. That contractor was killed in the parking garage of his apartment last week. And since Mr. Brisbane was seen arguing with him..."

Ms. Butters stared at her.

"That's absolutely ludicrous," she hissed. "That's slanderous. No one could possibly believe Mr. Brisbane had anything to do with that man's death."

Amirah took another bite of her sandwich and said casually, "I'll bet it would be easy to put an end to the rumors. All Mr. Brisbane has to do is make sure everyone knows where he was when the killing happened. You don't happen to know, do you? It was Wednesday evening around six-thirty, from what I've been told."

Ms. Butters hesitated, her mouth pinched into a sour frown, and then said, "I don't know why I'm telling you this, but I do know where he was on Wednesday evening. Earlier in the week, he had me make reservations for two at the Betruger, a German restaurant, for Wednesday at six p.m., for him and his fiancée. Dozens of people would have seen him there– Miss de Reis, the wait staff, the other diners…"

Amirah grinned. "Well, there you go, then. Problem solved."

As soon as she was in the lobby and out of sight of Ms. Butters, she pulled out her phone and shot off a long text to her husband.

Chapter 15

The young woman who opened the door at Mason's knock hung on it for a moment, arching her back to emphasize the braless chest beneath her Kate Moss T-shirt, and looked him carefully up and down.

"Hmm, not bad for an older guy. What is it you're selling again? Maybe I might be interested in buying some."

Mason raised his eyebrows. "Miss de Reis?"

At the same time, a voice came from inside the apartment: "Stop trying to molest the man, Brie, and show him in."

The girl flashed him a grin and extended her hand. "Brie Montgerard. It's my cousin Eva you're wanting to see. This way, sir."

He was in the fourth-floor entryway of a luxury apartment building on the east side of the city called The Slope, the home of Frederick Brisbane's fiancée. After some effort, he had passed the first hurdle, convincing the concierge to go to the trouble of calling upstairs to find out if the young woman would see him, and now it was time to face Miss de Reis herself.

The Slope was designed in the latest style, all spare lines and unexpected shapes, resembling in its general outline a giant furnace filter that someone had squeezed in the middle. As he was ushered into 4B, he saw that the interior of the apartment was decorated in the same vein.

Evangeline de Reis was waiting in the living room, in the center of an area rug with broad sweeps of color, with a glass of white wine in her hand. She was a strawberry blonde, slim without being angular, and her brown eyes looked him over guardedly. She was dressed in a heather-colored V-neck and fashionably-torn jeans, with a thin band of tiny diamonds in white gold around her neck. Despite the simplicity of her attire, Mason suspected that every single article of clothing he was wearing plus all the contents of his pockets wouldn't equal the cost of the least expensive item she had on.

She waved him to an armchair covered in copper circles and sat across from him on the sofa. Her cousin curled up on the far end of the sofa and immediately busied herself with her phone, but occasionally lifted her head to cast glances across at Mason.

"Care for anything to drink?" Eva asked. "No? So, how can I help you? You told Garfield, the concierge, that this is regarding my fiancé's work?"

"That's right." Mason held out his wallet so she could see his detective's license clearly. "In view of certain recent events, my agency, Gates and Gates Investigations, has been hired to clarify some points about the routine at CanCorp. It shouldn't take more than a few minutes of your time."

"Wouldn't it make more sense to ask Frederick these questions, since he's the one who works there?"

Mason gave her what he hoped was a disarming smile. "Sometimes it's best to approach these things in a roundabout way, I've found. Now, when does Mr. Brisbane usually arrive at work?"

"Seven o'clock."

"And what time does he normally leave work?"

"Around four or four-thirty, usually."

"So that by six p.m. he would be having supper? He wouldn't be at Canfield Tower at that time?"

"Hardly, unless some emergency came up–and considering he works in Marketing, those sorts of emergencies are few and far between."

"If I were to pick an evening at random, would you be able to say where he was then? Say this past Wednesday, for instance?"

Eva de Reis sat very still on the sofa and regarded him warily. "Frederick had dinner at the home of an old colleague from medical school Wednesday, and afterward stayed to play poker. That's been a custom of their group, Wednesday poker nights once or twice a month, for as long as they've known each other."

"Did you speak to him that evening?"

"No. I texted him around noon. I often do that on the days we don't lunch together, and he texted me just before he turned in for the night, but we didn't actually talk."

"I see. Could I get the name of this colleague of his?"

"Dr. Abel Raboy."

"Do you happen to know his address?"

She shook her head. "Frederick has it in his phone, of course, but I do know he works at St. Cosmas-Brookside."

"Thank you, Miss de Reis, I think that's everything."

Mason started to rise, but Eva put her glass down on the geometric table at her right hand and stopped him with an imperative gesture.

"You don't have any other questions for me? Then maybe you'll be so kind as to tell me what this is actually about. I'm not innocent enough to believe you'd come all the way here, without my fiancé's knowledge, simply to verify some unimportant details. Especially considering most of your questions were about how Frederick spent his evening, something that can't possibly be of real concern to his firm."

Mason perched on the edge of his armchair and nodded.

"You're right, Miss de Reis. There's more involved than basic security concerns. You probably weren't aware of this, but an independent contractor working for CanCorp was recently attacked and killed at his home, and there's a possibility that his death may be connected to the company. Certainly, whoever killed him was aware of his routine. Under the circumstances, Mr. Brisbane's superiors have some reservations regarding his relationship with the victim, and my job is simply to gather all the facts."

Brie lifted her head. "You're talking about that Middle Eastern guy who was stabbed in his apartment building, aren't you? It was all over the news this weekend. They said it was a hate crime."

Eva, her eyes fixed on Mason, asked, "What circumstances are you referring to?"

"Mr. Brisbane was overheard arguing with the victim shortly before he died. That, combined with his well-known views on individuals of certain backgrounds…"

Brie grimaced at her cousin. "You have to admit, Frederick is pretty right-wing, Eva. There are times when he sounds so much like your father, it's spooky."

Eva ignored her. "Should I even be talking to you about this, Mr. Gates, or should Frederick be contacting his lawyer?"

"As far as I know, no one's suggested that he actually had anything to do with this man's death. But it would be in his best interest to state clearly where he was when it happened, just so there are no misunderstandings."

"And this was on Wednesday evening?"

"Yes. Wednesday at six-thirty."

"I see. Thank you."

From The Slope, Mason headed to the south side of the city, to St. Cosmas-Brookside Hospital. It was a smaller facility with a weather-beaten exterior, which primarily handled patients from the low-income neighborhoods that surrounded it. He pulled into the parking lot outside the general entrance, then strolled inside and sat down unhurriedly in the lobby, taking advantage of the free Wi-Fi to look up Dr. Raboy. Having determined the doctor's field of practice, he took the elevator to the third floor, to the Neurology department.

The third-floor receptionist, after determining that he did not have an appointment and that his visit was not concerning a current patient, gave him a long-suffering look and stated that Dr. Raboy was very busy and it would be best to make an appointment. She thought he might have an opening in two and a half weeks.

Mason said, "Why don't you give him my card, and let him know this is regarding a personal matter, and should take only a few minutes."

She went off wearing the same expression, and returned shortly without the card Mason had given her.

"The doctor says he'll see you after he finishes with his current patient. It shouldn't be long. There's a waiting area outside his office. Go down the left-hand hallway here and take the first left, then on the right..."

Forty-five minutes later, the office door opened, and Mason lowered the two-month-old copy of *Field & Stream* he had been leafing through. Dr. Raboy, a slim man with curly black hair and an intense expression, ushered out his patient, a middle-aged woman supporting herself on a quad cane, and after a polite interval, called Mason's name. He settled himself behind his desk after waving the detective to a chair, and turned Mason's card over in his hands.

"Gloria said you told her this was regarding a personal matter. I can't think of a single circumstance in my life that would require the involvement of a private investigator."

"Good to hear. I'll get right to the point, Doctor. I know your time is valuable. I simply need your help determining the whereabouts of a certain individual at a certain time. Are you acquainted with a Frederick Brisbane Jr.?"

"I am."

"Was he at your house this past Wednesday evening for a poker game?"

"My place? Is that what he told you?" Raboy tossed the card onto his desk. "I haven't had Wednesday night poker at my place in over a year. Between my working double shifts and my wife taking care of our new twin girls, the only thing the two of us feel like doing in the evenings is crashing in front of the television. What's this all about? I'm really not interested in getting mixed up in some divorce case."

Mason noticed that the doctor said specifically "divorce case," and not simply "legal case." Since Brisbane wasn't married, and his friend would know that, it painted the executive's personality in a distinct light. He smiled at Raboy.

"This isn't that. But it is important for us to determine exactly where Mr. Brisbane was on Wednesday night. His story is that he had dinner with your family, then spent the rest of that evening at your home playing poker. I take it that wasn't the case?"

"Not even remotely. I haven't seen him for at least a couple of weeks, maybe even a month. To be frank, we don't get around in the same circles anymore. We started drifting apart after he left medical school."

"That was when he switched fields to marketing?"

"He may have gone into marketing afterward, but that wasn't why he left med school. He was asked to leave, for a combination of reasons."

"Problems with the opposite sex?" Mason guessed.

The doctor's answer confirmed his earlier suspicions.

Raboy sighed. "I suppose it's relevant to whatever you're investigating? For one, it came out that he was carrying on with two of our fellow students at the same time, which caused a bit of an uproar. Not that that sort of thing's unusual among doctors and nurses–and sadly, some of them never outgrow it. The second thing that came to light was his tendency to shortchange certain patients; to give quick, off-the-cuff diagnoses to ethnic patients so he wouldn't have to spend any more time with them than he had to."

"I see. So, to go back for a moment, would you have any idea where Frederick Brisbane might have been on Wednesday evening?"

"None at all."

"Do you know why he'd say he was at your house at the time?"

"Not a clue."

Mason rose and shook his hand. "Thank you, Doctor. I think I've just about got a good, clear impression now."

Chapter 16

Mason waited until he heard the double chirp of the car alarm before he approached, and until the man had his hand on the door handle before he spoke.

"Mr. Brisbane?"

Frederick Brisbane Jr. lifted his head and stared at him across the roof of his car. He was a year or two past forty, medium height and well-dressed, with wavy dark brown hair, a strong nose, and a full lower lip that probably looked attractive when he put forth the effort, but was petulant in repose.

"Do I know you?" he asked.

Mason held his open wallet up long enough for the businessman to get a brief glimpse of his PI license. "My name is Gates. I've been hired to look into certain matters related to Canfield Tower. I think it would be a good idea if we talked."

Brisbane hit the unlock button on his key fob again and tossed his attaché case on the back seat of the BMW. "Do you? Well, you can just contact my secretary and make an appointment, and I'll see if I can squeeze you in. I'm not in the habit of having business discussions in parking garages. Good day."

He slung himself behind the wheel of the car and slammed the driver's door. Mason swung open the front passenger door and sat quickly opposite him.

"Excuse me! What on earth do you think you're

doing? Do you want me to call security?"

Mason smiled thinly at him. He had been lurking in odd corners of the employee garage across from CanCorp for the past hour, holding a copy of the *Wall Street Journal* in front of him and hoping to avoid the attention of security before he had a chance to corner the Assistant Vice-President of Marketing.

"Before you pick up your phone, Mr. Brisbane, or put the car into gear, or do anything else, you might consider that sparing me a few minutes of your time now could avoid a good amount of unpleasantness later."

Brisbane glared at him. "Is that supposed to be a threat? Exactly what is this about, anyway?"

"Does the name Kadeem Nassar mean anything to you?"

Brisbane stared at him blankly. "Should it?"

"He was an independent contractor doing some sensitive work for your employers, and he was killed last week at his home. It's come to my attention that you were involved in at least one altercation with him, and considering the circumstances, you might want to explain what that was all about."

"I don't know what you're talking about."

"You're saying you never spoke to him?" Mason prodded.

"I really can't recall. Now if you'll excuse me–"

"Let me rephrase what I said before. You were witnessed, by multiple employees, having an argument with him in the company elevator. That fact isn't in dispute. Are you sure you don't want to get your side of the situation out in the open?"

"That was a private matter, between the two of us,"

Brisbane said and started to reach for the ignition button. "I don't have to answer your questions. In fact, I think it would be best if I contacted my lawyer before I say another word."

As a police officer, Mason had been able to rely for the most part on the authority of his badge to get answers to his questions, especially since he had worked directly for the district attorney's office. As a civilian investigator, he had no authority, and few people respected the work he did. He had quickly learned that persuasion and a reasonable manner were his best instruments.

He held up his hands. "You're right. You're not obligated to answer my questions. But before you make any rash decisions, you may want to think about this: I'm not a cop, and no one's recording this conversation. My job is simply to prepare a private report covering all aspects of the situation, a situation that could potentially have serious repercussions for your company. What do you suppose will look better in that report, that you refused to be of assistance, or that you answered my questions to the best of your ability? I can guarantee that when it comes down to it, a multi-billion-dollar corporation won't hesitate to cut loose an executive who puts his personal interests ahead of his loyalty to the company, no matter how many de Reis lawyers he may have behind him."

Brisbane, his face flushed, dropped his hand back in his lap.

"Thank you," Mason said blandly. "I always appreciate dealing with someone sensible. I can promise you, whatever you have to tell me will stay confidential, as long as it has no direct bearing on the death of Mr. Nassar."

"What do you want to know?" Brisbane asked.

"First off, tell me about the argument in the elevator. That seems like a good place to start."

Brisbane sighed. "I only crossed paths with Kadeem Nassar twice in the time he worked here. You swear these details won't end up in your report?" Mason nodded, and the businessman went on. "About two weeks ago, he happened to walk into one of the supply rooms and caught me in a compromising situation with one of the marketing interns. It was entirely consensual, I give you my word on that, and in the heat of the moment, neither of us remembered to lock the door behind us. I caught up with him in the hallway outside and told him to forget what he'd seen, that it was nobody's business but ours, and there was no point in his making ripples over something that wasn't hurting anyone.

"His response was not exactly reassuring. He shrugged off my hand on his arm and muttered something as he walked away. I tried to let it go, but what could I do? The last thing in the world I need is for my career at CanCorp to be torpedoed because HR gets wind of some office gossip. Several days later, we ended up in the back of the elevator together, and I leaned across and asked him if he'd thought about what I said. If he was going to keep his mouth shut. I couldn't believe what he said back to me. He told me not to try pushing him around or threatening him, that whether he told anyone about what'd happened or not was his decision, and I could just wait to find out what he'd decided.

"I was livid. He had absolutely no business talking

to me like that. We didn't invite those people to come here to this country just so they could act like they're better than us. Well, I kept my voice down, but I didn't hesitate to point out who I was and who he was, and that someone like him was fortunate to have a job here at all. I made it clear he didn't want to get on my bad side. And then he turned and shoved me, right there in the elevator, in front of everyone, like some hooligan! I suppose he couldn't help it, it's in their blood to act like savages, but it caught me off guard."

"What did you do?"

"Nothing. The elevator came to a stop just then and everyone started exiting, including him. I certainly wasn't about to start a fight with him right there in the lobby, so I let him go. I thought about contacting HR myself before he had a chance to, but considering everything involved I decided I'd give him some time to cool off first. And that's it. That was the last time I ever saw him. Are you satisfied?"

"Not quite," Mason said. "There are several details I'd like to clarify before we're finished. Let's back up a moment. You said the conversation outside the supply room happened about two weeks ago. You're sure it wasn't longer than that?"

"No, it was two, two and a half weeks ago. Somewhere around there, anyway."

"I see. Now on to another critical point. Nassar was killed Wednesday at approximately six-thirty p.m. Where were you then?" Before Brisbane could answer, Mason added, "If it makes things any simpler for you, I can tell you I've spent most of the afternoon crisscrossing the city, listening to people tell me where you weren't."

The executive stared at him, his mouth open, and it took a moment before he responded. Mason's blue-gray eyes regarded him steadily.

"All right, all right! If you absolutely have to know, I spent Wednesday evening with a friend."

"Starting with dinner reservations at the Betruger?"

"You know about that? Yes, fine. We had dinner at the Betruger and then went to a hotel. I was with her till about eleven."

"Was this friend the intern you mentioned earlier?"

"No, no, someone else."

"Her name? Details, Mr. Brisbane."

Brisbane sighed gustily, exasperated. "You really mean to dig up everything, don't you? There's no possible way this has any connection with what happened to that contractor... For God's sake! All right. Her name is Marla Sturges, she's married, and we see each other one or two times a month, on Wednesday evenings."

"What hotel did you go to?"

"The Durbridge Motel. It isn't far from the subdivision where she lives, and she can make it home by midnight. Is there anything else you want to know?"

"Just your opinion on what happened to Nassar. Since you didn't have anything more to do with him after your argument in the elevator, can you think of anyone else at CanCorp who might have borne him a grudge?"

"You want me to play whistle-blower now, is that it? As a matter of fact, I do have an idea about who you should be investigating. Gerome Westbrook, one of the managers in Accounting."

"Why him particularly?"

"Everyone knew why this Nassar was brought in. To reorganize the accounting department, to help clear out the dead wood, maybe even replace one of the existing managers. The accounting department has to meet performance quotas just like every other department here, and lately, they haven't been doing so well. In my opinion, Westbrook's got to be the one to go–he's missed work multiple times over the past few months, and if he keeps that up, well…"

"So you think he might've killed Nassar to keep him from taking over his position?"

"Why not?"

"Right. Why not? Thanks." Mason reached for his door handle. "Cheer up, Mr. Brisbane. As long as everything you've told me is true, there's no reason you should ever have to see me again."

Chapter 17

As the film credits began to scroll up the screen, Amirah swung around on the couch and dropped her bare feet onto her husband's lap. Mason obligingly held his bowl of popcorn up out of the way.

"So," she asked, "what do you think of our Assistant Vice-President of Marketing?"

"Mr. Frederick Brisbane Jr.? Well, he had a motive of sorts, and with his medical background, it's possible he'd have access to a scalpel or something like it and the know-how to use it lethally…"

Amirah, reading her husband's expression, said, "But?"

"I'm pretty certain he's not the person we're looking for. He told his secretary he was with his fiancée Wednesday evening. He told his fiancée he was staying over at a friend's house that night. He told me he spent the evening with a married woman. If I question her, chances are good she'll deny it and tell me he was somewhere else then. It's the sort of multitude of lies you'd expect from a man having an affair, but it's a lousy way of setting up an alibi for murder.

"Not that I didn't cross my t's and dot my i's. I stopped at the Betruger this evening just before the dinner crowd started showing up and asked as many questions as the maître d' would let me get away with. It's a very exclusive place, seating by reservation only, and naturally, they don't want to discuss their customers with any old stranger, but with enough folding persuasion–"

"You mean you had to pay him for information? Dare I ask how much?"

Mason made a face. "Better if you don't. But don't worry–it'll go down on our tax forms as a business expense."

"I wouldn't expect any less. And what did you learn?"

"Frederick Brisbane Jr. is a regular at the Betruger, and was definitely there on Wednesday night, during the time of Kadeem Nassar's murder, with a young woman. Not Evangeline de Reis. This woman was a sandy brunette with platinum highlights."

"So he's out of the running." Amirah pushed another pillow behind her and scooped a fistful of popcorn from her bowl. "How did you manage to find out where his fiancée lives? I'm sure she's not listed in the phone book."

Mason ran the tip of his forefinger up the inside of her calf. "Everything's on the Internet, babe. It's only a matter of looking. I just searched for street photos of Evangeline de Reis, and there she was, caught in the act of leaving her building."

"Clever man. So as far as we can tell, the police's prime suspect is a dud, and our one and only suspect is a dud. Where do we go from here?"

Mason's hand drifted past her kneecap. "You didn't hear anything else interesting while you were at CanCorp today?"

"Not a thing. Kadeem seems to have kept to himself, which was exactly what he was told to do.

Good for him, but not so good for us."

Mason shrugged. "So you keep doing what you're doing, poking around for anything that sounds like a clue. There's no rushing it. In the meantime–"

His fingers slipped under the hem of her nightshirt, and she gave a little yelp of pleasant surprise. As his other hand slid around her waist and pulled her toward him, she thrust her bowl of popcorn onto the coffee table, out of his way, spilling half the leftover kernels in the process.

Fifty-five minutes went by before either of them noticed.

\*\*\*\*

When she entered Janeen Walkowitz's office the next morning, Amirah had a plan of action: since the accounting head had explained everything that was known about the embezzlement the previous day, and since she was there under the guise of being a temp, why not have her sit in with one of the accounting teams, and see what information she could pick up that way?

The accounting head, who today was wearing a lapel pin of Snoopy as Joe Cool, placed her hands flat on her desk and nodded.

"Whatever you think is best. Have you discovered something you want to follow up on?"

Amirah smiled and shrugged. "No, I'm sorry. We're still at the fishing phase of our investigation."

"I see. Follow me, then."

Ms. Walkowitz led her out into the main work area, where the accountants' cubicles were located. As they skirted the perimeter, Amirah realized the cubicles were arranged roughly in the shape of a cross, with each set of workspaces oriented toward one of the outer walls, facing the office of the manager for that particular division. They stopped at the office of the Southeast manager, Gerome Westbrook, and Ms. Walkowitz explained that she was going to have Amirah spend some time with his team.

Westbrook, who looked to be about ten years older than Amirah, had a pinched face and thinning brown hair. He lifted his head from the papers in front of him with a distracted expression.

"Fine, that's fine."

He made no effort to rise from his desk, and the accounting head had to take Amirah out and introduce her to the four members of his team. Amirah spent the rest of the morning with a notepad and pen balanced on her knee, learning about the various accounts the company managed: retirement funds, investment portfolios, estate planning, trust funds, stocks and bonds—the list went on. Whenever one of the firm's brokers met with a client and set up a new account, or helped make a change from one type of account to another, the account request was sent over to the team for that particular region, and the account was finalized and activated.

"Now," said the young woman named Charlie, whose straight black hair was tucked behind ears with multiple hoops in them, "even though we can activate accounts all day long, only a manager or higher can make an account inactive."

"It's a customer service thing," added Toby, a stocky youth with thick-framed glasses. "The managers reach out to the clients before they close an account, to make sure they can't get them to change their mind, or see if there's some other service they might need instead."

Charlie added, "We also make sure the clients get all the bells and whistles with their accounts, like email or text alerts. We can even set them so they get alerts every single time there's a deposit or withdrawal–but speaking personally, I think that'd drive me nuts after a while."

"What do you think of the job itself?" Amirah asked. "Are the benefits good?"

"Oh, sure," answered Kumal, who had sleek black hair and a stubbly beard. "We have full medical and dental here, an hour for lunch, prorated vacation days, a great retirement plan–but to be honest, a person's only going to stick around in this department if they really love numbers. That's basically all we do all day, move numbers around."

"Come on, there's more to it than that!" laughed the fourth team member, Lana, and ran her hand through her ash-blond-streaked hair. "But yeah, you've got to love it, or you won't last long."

"What about the managers?" asked Amirah. "I met all four of them yesterday, but only briefly. How are they to work for?"

"Mr. Westbrook, our manager, is decent," said Kumal. "We don't get too many complaints from him, and he usually tries to work with us whenever there's an issue."

It was only a coincidence that the first accounting team she had ended up with was overseen by Gerome Westbrook, the individual Frederick Brisbane Jr. had implicated when Mason was questioning him, but Amirah didn't intend to let the opportunity to learn about him slip by.

"Is he the one who's been missing a lot of work lately? Someone mentioned his name the other day…"

Lana nodded and lowered her voice a notch. "Something's going on with him. He's been out a lot in the last couple of months, using up his sick days and vacation days."

"What do you think is the reason?" Amirah asked. "Family problems? Financial problems?"

Toby smirked at her last suggestion. "Whatever it is, it isn't money problems. Mr. Westbrook comes from old money. Heck, his dad is golfing buddies with the CEO of the company."

"You mean Jerald Canfield?"

"No, no, Mr. Canfield's the president. Mr. Nederostek is the CEO."

Amirah's eyes widened. "What's the difference? I thought Mr. Canfield was in charge of everything. Isn't he? I mean, the company is named after him, isn't it?"

Kumal smiled knowingly. "His family started the company, and they own a big share of it still, but he isn't the one at the top. The big, big boss is Laurence Nederostek, the CEO, who oversees the company's long-range strategies and profits, and so on. Mr. Canfield drops in here from time to time, and puts in an appearance at all the company functions, but from what I hear, Mr. Nederostek attends board meetings, and that's about it. For him to show up in person is like Zeus coming down from Mount Olympus."

"I see," Amirah said, and scribbled several notes on her notepad. "So what about the other managers? What are they like?"

"Ms. Atchison's nice," said Lana. "Mr. deWitt's all

business. I've never seen him crack a smile. Then again, I've never worked for him. He may be a real party animal at heart, who knows? Mr. Fathy–"

"Mr. Fathy is a hands-off kind of manager," Kumal said. "He spends most of his time in his office and deals with his team by email generally."

"Have you ever seen any of them lose their cool? Or get into fights with employees?"

Kumal stared at Amirah. "I don't know where you've worked before, but that kind of thing doesn't happen at CanCorp."

"Well, I wouldn't say that," objected Charlie. "There was that commotion in the elevator the other day, remember? But that wasn't one of our managers, that was one of the Marketing bigwigs. He got in a shoving match with an independent contractor. No clue what it was all about."

"I heard it was over a woman," Lana said. "And wasn't it the same contractor that was working with Ms. Walkowitz recently?"

Charlie shrugged and, catching Amirah's eye, shook her head dismissively. "Maybe it was, maybe it wasn't. You know how rumors get started in a place like this…"

At lunchtime, the Southeast team ordered in: sub sandwiches from Bonner's, a regional favorite. Amirah chose a pastrami cheesesteak, an unusual combination that was known to draw people from across the state. Outside of the Bonner's chain, it was said, the nearest places to find a comparable sandwich were Philadelphia and Anchorage.

Her phone buzzed in the middle of lunch, and she took a quick slurp of her soda to wash down the mouthful of sandwich. It was her sister Aziza.

"Hi, Zee. What's up?"

"Amirah, are you busy?" Aziza asked, and as usual, swept on without giving her a chance to respond. "I have another idea for our parents' anniversary party I want to run by you."

"Not another lavish cake concept, I hope?"

"No, no. I decided you were right about the cake. We're going to have *qatayef* instead. *Baba* will be much more pleased with that." *Qatayef*, a filled dessert halfway between a pancake and a dumpling, was a favorite dish in the region where their father had grown up. "No, I have a brilliant idea for the music during the party. There's a musician here in the city, Syrian-born, who heads a group that's available for special events. They call themselves Sheik Agha, and they play traditional Middle Eastern music, on traditional instruments. They even dress in authentic costumes. Wouldn't it be fantastic to have them perform for the evening?"

Amirah sighed. "Will you do me a favor, Aziza? Ask one of our aunts, any one of them, what they think *baba* would think of that idea. Then, when you've heard what they have to say, you can ask me again."

"Amirah! Why ever would I do a thing like that? This party is supposed to be a surprise. If I go blabbing to all our aunts about it…"

After several excruciating minutes of listening to her sister ramble on, Amirah finally ended the call, to find the others watching her. She grinned at their curious expressions. To explain she only had to say one word: "Family!"

She spent the rest of the day with the Northeast

team, but without learning anything especially noteworthy. When they went home at four o'clock, she returned to Janeen Walkowitz's office to find the auditor from CAA, George, standing at the folding table in the corner, clicking his briefcase shut.

"Any luck?" she asked.

"Nothing so far," said Ms. Walkowitz, waving briefly to the departing accountant. "We're bound to find something eventually–we have to–but it's probably going to take us another two months to work our way back to wherever Mr. Nassar was when he died."

Amirah stood stock still as the other woman's words struck her. "You're starting over from the beginning? My agency still has the laptop Kadeem used in his work. We haven't assumed his killer and your embezzler are the same person, because we didn't want to overlook any possibilities–but let's say they are. If Kadeem was killed because he stumbled across information pointing to the theft, wouldn't that information be in the last account he worked on, or one of the last? If we can access the accounts he was looking at…"

She pulled out her phone and dialed her cousin Sa'id's number.

"Sa'id? It's Amirah. Are you where you can get to that laptop we left you? We need to find out what the victim was working on last."

A few minutes passed, while Sa'id talked to himself on the other end of the connection. Finally, he said: "I've got his history up, but all it tells me is he logged into the CanCorp system. I could remote into it if I had his username and password, maybe find out what you want to know that way."

Amirah turned to the accounting head. "You wouldn't happen to know Kadeem's login ID to the company network, would you?"

Ms. Walkowitz opened her top drawer and quickly retrieved a small spiral-bound notebook.

"I have it right here," she said. "I thought it might be a good idea to keep a record of it myself. Ordinarily, passwords are the province of the IT department, but not knowing just who to trust at the moment... The username is knassar98, no capitals, the password is 'mutarada.' Do you need me to spell that for you?"

"I've got it," Amirah said with a smile. *Mutarada* was "hunt" in Arabic. She conveyed the information to her cousin.

"Got it," he said. "I'm in now. Looking for the activity log... Found it. I have a list of accounts here. You want the most recent one first, I guess?"

He read off the nine-digit account number, while Amirah held the phone out so Ms. Walkowitz could hear him.

"Did you get that?" she asked.

The accounting head nodded, and her fingers tapped rapidly at her keyboard. "I'm looking at it now. The account's inactive, which is odd. I don't know why Mr. Nassar would've been looking at an inactive account, but I can make it active again, and we can review the history."

Amirah thanked her cousin and dropped her phone in her purse, and coming around the desk, looked over the other woman's shoulder.

"It looks like the account was just closed this past Friday–"

"The day after Kadeem was killed," Amirah said

tautly.

"And the balance was transferred, probably to a bank account, since the routing number isn't one of our internal ones. The balance at that point was slightly over sixty-four thousand dollars. And now look at the deposit history... a continuous stream of ten cent deposits, stretching back for who knows how long... This is it, it has to be! Mr. Nassar found the key account, the one our thief's been funneling money into."

Amirah frowned at the computer screen. "Is there anything about the account that could give us a clue to the person responsible?"

"Let's see... Customer name, Joel Tilton, from Estes Park, Colorado..."

"Probably plucked out of the phone book," Amirah muttered.

"The account was opened eight years ago... Oh, look at this. Here's a tip-off, if I'd ever happened to see it. You notice the Social Security number entered for Mr. Tilton?"

Amirah looked closely at the screen and then stared at her blankly.

"It's a fake. No Social Security number has consecutive zeroes. If nothing else proves it, that definitely proves this is a dummy account."

"And you can't tell where the money was transferred to from here?"

"Not without some research. Normally, the commentary line, whether for a deposit or a withdrawal, contains a routing number, an account number, and some kind of descriptor to help us and the client know what transaction took place. We have the expected numbers, but in this case, the only descriptor on the withdrawals is 'BDFN.' It'll take some time for us to figure out what that stands for."

Amirah straightened up, her large eyes gleaming. "So Kadeem Nassar pinned down the embezzlement scheme."

"Yes. At least, it's the first, solid corner of the whole thing." Ms. Walkowitz logged off of her computer and put it to sleep. "There's a lot of work ahead of us. We're going to have to follow each individual deposit back and plug every leak, reimburse our clients their funds, then follow the trail forward and see if we can determine where the stolen money is now and how we can go about getting it back. Not to mention continuing to look for any other dummy accounts–and considering the one we just saw, it looks like we're going to have to broaden the search to all the inactive accounts, as well. It's going to take some time."

They walked out to the elevators together. By that time most of the staff of the forty-first floor were gone. Apart from a few managers here and there, the hallways were quiet. Stockbrokers' schedules, Amirah was learning, revolved around New York Stock Exchange hours, and for those who lived west of the Mississippi, that led to some early days. The brokers at CanCorp were generally out of the building by two o'clock or two-thirty, while the accountants rarely stayed past four.

As they rode down to the ground floor, Ms. Walkowitz broke the silence by making casual conversation. What they had just discovered regarding the embezzlement led to enough further questions that it seemed pointless to discuss it then. Instead, the older woman, who had struck Amirah as very businesslike before, surprised her by chatting at length about her two very talkative cockatiels and her hobby of raising various rare plants in her home.

Their heels echoed in the mostly-empty lobby as they crossed to the main entrance, and the guard at the central desk watched them pass with a bored expression.

They emerged through one of the multiple revolving doors into a soft late afternoon breeze. They were in a lull before the other glass-and-steel honeycombs let out their employees at five, and passing cars were few and far between. They crossed the open space in front of Canfield Tower at a diagonal, headed for the corner and the crosswalk that would take them over to the company parking garage on the opposite block.

While they waited for the light to change, they discussed their respective dinner plans and the best place in the city to get a porterhouse. The street parallel to them was one-way in their direction, and a small part of Amirah's mind noticed a light-colored car facing them, parked at the curb just past the garage entrance. She wondered why it was sitting there, halfway into the yellow no-parking zone leading to the corner. Surely it wasn't just because there were no available spaces in the garage?

The traffic light turned green, and the little figure appeared in the signal box. They stepped off the curb, still talking.

The car facing them pulled away from the curb at the same time, and the driver, apparently in a hurry, floored it. The car surged forward, tires squealing, and swung in a wide left-handed arc directly into the crosswalk.

Amirah stopped and held her arm out to restrain the other woman. She wasn't overly concerned; the avenue they were crossing had four lanes, and there was plenty of room for the driver to pass if they simply stood still where they were.

The instant that thought occurred to her, it was followed by another: the car was not going to pass. It was headed straight for them.

What happened then happened very quickly, in a matter of seconds.

There was no time to step out of the way, no time to walk or even run for the curb. When she saw the front of the car rushing toward them, Amirah wrenched herself around and jumped, at the same time shoving Ms. Walkowitz as hard as she could with both hands.

The car swept past with only an inch or two to spare, the hot air of its passage whipping over them and its near-side tires almost mounting the curb.

Amirah found herself sitting sprawled on the sidewalk, her heart pounding in her chest, as the vehicle sped away down the street. She stared after it while she caught her breath, then turned to Ms. Walkowitz, who was lying on her side facing the other direction. Amirah helped her to sit up; long scrapes on the older woman's temple and cheek were beginning to seep scarlet.

Behind them was the pounding of rubber soles on pavement as a pair of Canfield Tower guards came running to their aid. Amirah fished a tissue from her purse and pressed it gingerly to the other woman's face.

Ms. Walkowitz said dazedly, "That– that car came

straight at us… The driver–he was trying to run us down!"

"Oh, yes," Amirah said matter-of-factly, surprising herself by how steady her voice was. "The only question is, which of us was he aiming for, you or me?"

Chapter 18

By the time Mason Gates reached Canfield Tower the avenue in front of it was lined with vehicles.

He had been heading back to the office to finish up some paperwork and wait for Amirah when he got her text. It had comprised only a few words: —Incident here at CT. Come get me.—

Just enough information to elevate his blood pressure, and not enough to limit his imagination once it got going. The drive across town only gave him opportunity to stew.

He pulled his car to a hard stop and flung himself out, not bothering to shut the driver's-side door, and strode rapidly past a black Mercedes SUV and two of three squad cars to the ambulance at the center of it all, sidestepping the officer that moved in his direction. Amirah and Ms. Walkowitz were sitting on the back of the ambulance, looking flushed, banged up, and a little disconcerted. An EMT was finishing securing a bandage over the latter woman's temple.

A uniformed patrolman flipped his notebook shut and turned away from the ambulance as Mason approached, eyeing him warily.

"What's going on?" Mason demanded. "Are you all right?"

In a time of crisis, the questions are banal, but the answers are so very important. Amirah lifted her large eyes to her husband's face with a mixture of relief and sheepishness.

"We're okay, sweetheart, really we are. Just a little scraped up and rattled."

"Are you sure? Positive?"

"Yes, I promise we are. Everything's fine now."

"Well, what happened?"

Amirah stood and looped her arms around Mason, leaning her head against his chest. "I just got through describing the whole thing to the police. I'll tell you everything, I will, but let's wait until we get away from here and my nerves have a chance to get back to normal, huh?"

Before Mason could say anything, there was the sound of footsteps behind him. He turned his head to see the president of CanCorp, Jerald Canfield IV, approaching, flanked by one of his brawny security men. The patrolman with the notebook made an attempt to cut them off.

"Sir, this is a potential crime scene. I'm going to need you and your associate to move back onto the sidewalk–"

"Have you finished taking these ladies' statements?" Canfield asked.

"Yes, sir, but–"

"Then there's no reason why we can't talk to them, is there?"

With that, the executive turned his back on the patrolman and ignored him. The man started to protest, but another officer caught him by the arm and whispered something in his ear, probably an explanation of who Canfield was, and he fell silent.

Canfield saw the question in Mason's eyes and

stepped closer to answer it, lowering his voice so that only they could hear him.

"Ever since this embezzlement came to light, I've had standing orders for Security to notify me the instant anything out of the ordinary happens here at Canfield Tower, no matter how small. As soon as they realized two of the building's employees were involved, they communicated with my staff, and I had my driver get me here as quickly as possible. How are you, Janeen? I'm assuming, since you're sitting upright, that you weren't seriously injured?"

"No, no, just some scratches and bruises." The accounting head grimaced. "I'll probably look lovely by tomorrow."

"And you, er, Miss?" he asked Amirah.

"The same," she replied.

"What exactly happened? The security team said the two of you were involved in a hit-and-run–or should I say, an almost-hit-and-run?"

"He only missed us by a few inches," Ms. Walkowitz said, and struck her fist lightly against her thigh. "We've managed to catch someone's attention! We found the dummy account the embezzler was using–or rather, Mr. Nassar discovered it before he was killed, and we re-discovered it. We've taken a solid step forward in finding the guilty party–and someone isn't happy about it."

Canfield regarded her thoughtfully. "So this was an attempt to run you over in response to that discovery? You're certain about that? You've determined the embezzler and Mr. Nassar's killer are definitely the same person?"

Ms. Walkowitz glanced at the two detectives,

whose faces were noncommittal. "I mean–it has to be the case, doesn't it?"

Canfield furrowed his brow. "There are aspects to this I'm not clear on yet. Granting for the sake of argument that the same person is responsible for both crimes, how would he know to be waiting for you to reach the street when he did? He couldn't have known when you planned to leave for the day. Unless you're suggesting he's been watching your office somehow and waiting for an opportunity like this?"

Mason, who had his hand on his wife's side, felt her tense up and gave her ribs a quick squeeze before she could respond.

"Those are excellent questions, Mr. Canfield," he said, "and we'll need some time to discuss them before we can give you an answer. In the meantime, I think we should let the ladies get home and recover from their ordeal, don't you?"

"Mmm, yes, of course."

"I'll get my car," Amirah said to her husband, "and then I can follow you back to the office–or you can follow me–"

"Forget the car," he said. "I can send Trick or Cecilia for it later. You're coming with me."

"Yes, that's a good idea," responded Canfield. "Janeen, I'll have my driver drop you off at your home, and one of the security men can follow us with your car."

The Gateses headed toward Mason's sedan. A patrolman stepped into their path.

"I'm sorry, sir, but you're going to have to move your vehicle. It's blocking traffic–"

"Don't worry, we're taking care of that right now."

When they were in the car, Amirah said, "Let's not go home yet, babe. After all this, I'm in no mood to think about what we're going to fix for dinner–that is, assuming I'll even have an appetite in an hour. Can't we just find a restaurant with a nice quiet corner somewhere?"

"I know exactly the spot," Mason said and headed to an Italian restaurant a little southeast of Canfield Tower called the Via Appia. It was a small, intimate place furnished in dark woods and crisp white linen, and he had them seated in a corner booth for additional privacy. When the waiter took their drink order, Amirah surprised her husband by asking for a glass of red wine.

When the drinks arrived, she let Mason do the rest of the ordering, veal piccata for him and shrimp scampi for her. As soon as the waiter had filled her glass, she grabbed at it and swallowed at least half its contents, then leaned back in her seat with a heavy sigh.

Mason contemplated her with raised eyebrows.

"Not a word!" she said. "What my father doesn't know won't hurt him. And I needed that."

"So," he began, "just what–"

"Oh, no. I'm going to need to recuperate some before I go over the whole thing. I think the reaction is kicking in. My hands are shaky, my tailbone is sore, and it feels like I pulled a muscle in my side."

Mason didn't say anything more; he simply reached across the table and took her hand. She looked into his gray-blue eyes gratefully.

It wasn't until their meals had been brought, between bites of shrimp and noodles, that she recounted the narrow escape she and Ms. Walkowitz had just had.

"Did you notice anything particular about the car

or the driver?" Mason asked when she finished.

She repeated what she had told the police. "It was a light gray four-door sedan. I wasn't paying any real attention to what kind of car it was, and I didn't get the license number. I'm pretty sure the driver was a man, someone with dark hair and sunglasses... Some detective I am, huh?"

He smiled reassuringly at her and reached across once again to squeeze her hand. "It was unexpected, and probably over in thirty seconds. You did as well as about anyone else would have under the circumstances... So, is this incident connected with the attack on Kadeem Nassar or not? If it is, what prompted the killer to strike now? If it isn't, what could be behind it? And in either case, the question Jerald Canfield asked is key–how did the driver of the car know when the two of you were going to emerge from Canfield Tower?"

"I know the answer to that one!" Amirah leaned forward eagerly. "Listen. I spent the entire day at CanCorp and didn't uncover any facts that pointed directly to a certain person or advanced our investigation. The only noteworthy thing that happened all day happened after four o'clock, when the accounting teams went home and I went back to Ms. Walkowitz's office. While I was there, with my cousin Sa'id's help, we found a dummy account the embezzler was using, the last account Kadeem was working on before he was killed. It'd been closed since his death, and she reactivated it so we could look at the account activity. Now I learned earlier today that some of the accounts are set up to provide account holders with alerts whenever there's activity of any sort. The embezzler must have gotten an alert on his–or her– phone saying the account had been reactivated, realized Ms. Walkowitz was responsible, and decided to eliminate her before she could get on his trail, just like he eliminated Kadeem. That car wasn't aiming for me, it was aiming for her. I just happened to be in the way."

"That's a relief to know," Mason responded wryly. "I was starting to rethink this idea of having you go undercover. In fact, I may still pull the plug on it. We're dealing with someone who's killed once. There's no telling how many times he'll try again before he's caught, and the next time we may not be so fortunate."

Amirah's eyes went perfectly round as she protested.

"Oh, no, I'm not quitting now, just when we're starting to make progress!"

Mason put down his forkful of veal and capers. "Baby, I know how you are. Once you start something, you want to follow it through all the way to the end. It's an admirable quality, but it could also be a fatal one, and what kind of husband would I be if I didn't think of my wife's welfare first? You're absolutely sure this wasn't an attempt on your life?"

"No, there's no chance. As far as anyone at CanCorp knows, I'm just a temp who's barely begun to learn the ropes. There'd be no reason for anyone to want me out of the picture. There's even a very slim chance it was just a random incident with a really bad driver–but an attack on me? Not possible."

"All right." Mason laughed and held up his hands in mock surrender. "I withdraw any suggestion of taking you off the case. But how can we be certain the embezzler and the person who killed Kadeem Nassar are the same person?"

"It fits. It all fits together," she said. "The dummy account was closed and emptied the very next day after Kadeem was killed. The same afternoon we rediscover and reactivate the account, someone tries to run Janeen Walkowitz over. Tell me that's not a solid connection."

"So you think–"

"I think the embezzler, who works in the accounting department, watched Ms. Walkowitz's office until it looked like we were leaving, hurried to the company parking garage for his car, and waited at that intersection until we emerged onto the street. It could only have been a spur-of-the-moment plan."

"You almost sound as if you have a certain person in mind."

"Not exactly, but does one out of four sound like a good number? I learned this morning that even though anyone in the accounting department can open an account, the number of people who can close an account is strictly limited. Only someone at managerial level or above–in other words, Ms. Walkowitz or one of the four regional managers. That's it. They do that for customer service reasons. Now if the account had been closed by anyone other than the embezzler, that person would have tried to reach out to the account holder, and would have quickly discovered said account holder doesn't exist, and the fake account would've been brought to light already. The only way it could've remained hidden until now is if it was closed by the person we're looking for. Obviously, Ms. Walkowitz isn't involved, so that leaves us with the four managers. Our killer just managed to draw the circle of suspicion tight around himself."

Mason smiled broadly with pride. "Nice. Now we're getting somewhere. What do you know about these regional managers?"

"I met all four of them yesterday morning, briefly. I can give you my impressions of them, but I haven't learned a lot about any of them so far."

"That's your focus from here on out, then. Find out as much as you can about them: backgrounds, addresses, type of cars they drive, any suspicious activity in recent weeks. Anything and everything you can."

Amirah nodded. Once finished with the meal, she pushed her empty plate away and leaned back against the seat cushions again, her eyelids lowered in weariness.

"I have a question for you, something that's been rattling around at the back of my mind. We know the killer is someone with a knowledge of anatomy, to be able to stab Kadeem Nassar straight to the heart like he did. Why not just cut his throat? Wouldn't that have been simpler?"

"Maybe," Mason said, "but it would've been a lot messier. And since one method wouldn't't've been any more difficult than the other to someone with experience, I'd imagine the killer simply chose the one that let him get away quickly and with the least fuss."

Amirah nodded but seemed not to be paying particular attention to the answer. Her lids were almost touching over her pale hazel eyes when they abruptly flew open and she sat bolt upright. Mason looked on in surprise as a dark flush crept across her cheeks.

"Oh my gosh! It just hit me. After it all happened, I was sitting there splayed across the sidewalk, and anybody passing by could have seen clear up my skirt. That's what I needed, for the whole world to see what kind of panties I have on!"

Mason lowered his head and poked at the remnants of his food with an innocent expression. "Bikini cut?"

She leaned across the table and punched his bicep playfully. "No, but they are bright lemon yellow. Probably visible all the way across the street."

"Well," he said slowly, "it seems to me the only thing to do–purely to ease your mind, of course–would be for me to take you home and make a careful examination for myself."

Amirah smirked at him. "In that case, Mr. Gates, don't you think you'd better hurry up and call for the check?"

Chapter 19

Amirah's first action the following morning was to stop at Janeen Walkowitz's home to make sure nothing had happened to her during the night, and to drive her to work. Mason had pointed out, after they had discussed it further, that if the killer now had the accounting head in his or her sights, they had to make her safety a priority, even if that limited the amount of sleuthing Amirah was able to do.

The ride into the financial district was an awkward one. Amirah tried to make conversation once or twice, but Ms. Walkowitz was understandably preoccupied with the previous day's incident and its implications, and her responses were short.

When they reached the forty-first floor of Canfield Tower, Amirah had her pull up the complete names and addresses of the four regional managers, and sent those off in a text to her husband so Mason could do some investigating of his own.

She then had Ms. Walkowitz take her around to sit in with the North accounting team. The North manager was a woman in her thirties named Samantha Atchison, a little taller than Amirah, with fluffy blond hair and a cheerful smile. "Call me Sammi," she said as they shook hands.

The North team was made up of three individuals: Jess, who was tall and lean, with her brown hair pulled back in a ponytail; Walt, whose round face was capped by rimless bifocals; and Maggie-Ann, short and curvy like Amirah, who favored multicolored ribbons in her blond hair and cartoon characters on the ends of her pencils. Amirah made sure the seat she took in their workspace had a clear view of Janeen Walkowitz's door.

She started out by asking them the same question she had asked the Southeast team, what they thought of the different managers.

"I don't know about the others," answered Jess, "but I don't think you could find a better manager than Ms. Atchison. She's almost always pleasant and sunny, no matter what kind of day she's having, and she's willing to stop what she's doing and pitch in if one of us needs help…"

"Which is surprising," added Maggie-Ann in her southern drawl, "considering the struggles she's had. She's divorced and raising two teenage boys on her own, and she put herself through night school to learn accounting and get a position here at CanCorp. Leastways, that's what I've been told. I don't know that I'd be so warm and friendly if I was juggling all that."

"What about the other managers?" Amirah asked. "I met Mr. Westbrook yesterday. I didn't talk to him much, but I got the impression he has a lot on his mind."

"He's definitely worried about something," Walt said, "and your guess what it is is as good as ours. He's missed a lot of work in the past couple of months. Used up almost all of his vacation time, I've heard."

"You don't have any idea what it could be about?"

None of them did. "Whatever it is," Jess said, "he's

kept it to himself."

"And the others?" Amirah asked. "I haven't met either of them yet."

"Mr. deWitt is the tell-it-like-it-is type," Jess replied. "He takes his job very seriously."

"Military background," added Walt. "You'll know what I mean when you see him. He keeps his hair buzzed short, like he's still in the Marines or something."

Amirah eyed the man's receding hairline and closely-trimmed hair and said nothing.

"The other manager, Mr. Fathy, nobody sees much of," said Maggie-Ann. "He's from the Middle East somewheres and only been in this country a few years. I think maybe he's just not comfortable around folks here yet."

"Have you ever heard of any of the managers having problems with certain employees?" Amirah asked.

Again she got a negative response. It seemed the North team members had little else to tell her about the upper levels at CanCorp.

Later, after a couple of hours of watching them activate and adjust various accounts, she noticed the coffee mug sitting on Walt's desk, dark olive with a stylized red throwing star on the side and the words SHURIKAN DEFENSE in red under it. Just to make conversation, she said, "That's interesting. Where did you get it?"

"Oh, this?" He grinned. "I ordered this from a catalog Mr. deWitt had. He's into those sorts of things, military gear and self-defense products, and he always has their catalogs on hand."

"Just about half of us here've ordered something from one of his catalogs one time or another," piped up Maggie-Ann. "Look."

She took the ring of keys from her purse and held it up. Among the various articles hanging from it was a metal piece in the shape of a cat's head, painted pink, with sharply-pointed ears and holes where the eyes would be.

"It's for self-defense," she explained. "You just slip your fingers in through the eyes, and jab! You give a mugger a taste of that, and you can believe he won't stick around."

"And you say Mr. deWitt has these catalogs here at work?"

"Oh, sure," Walt answered. "I wouldn't be surprised if he isn't on their website when he's in between tasks, checking out the latest products."

Amirah pressed her lips together thoughtfully, and when breaktime came, she slipped across to Janeen Walkowitz's office. The auditor from CAA, George, was busy at the folding table in the corner; at least with him present, she wasn't worried that the killer would make another attempt on the accounting head's life– although it was admittedly a pretty small chance any attempt would be made in the middle of a crowded office building.

"Is there any way," she asked, "you could call Mr. deWitt away from his office for a few minutes?"

Ms. Walkowitz stared steadily at her. "Should I ask what this is about?"

Amirah shrugged. "It might not be anything. I won't have any idea until afterward."

"So maybe the less I know, the better," Ms.

Walkowitz said ruefully, and reached for her telephone. "I'll think of something to keep him here for a little bit... Hello, Matt? Can you come to my office for a minute? Thank you."

Amirah stepped out into the corridor as the North manager approached, and after he'd entered Ms. Walkowitz's office, she spun around and hurried along to his. Her heartbeat raced. Any moment she expected someone to call out to her and arrest her in her steps, probably deWitt himself.

She reached his office, located in the back left corner of the main work area, and with a sweep of her head to check for observers, she eased inside.

She had to move quickly, before deWitt returned to his office and caught her. She was looking for a physical copy of the self-defense catalog she had been told about. She hoped fervently that he had one in his office, or else she'd have to try looking on his computer for a link or a bookmark that would take her to the company's website, and that would take a good deal longer–if his computer wasn't locked to her entirely.

If it was anywhere, it would be near at hand, somewhere in or on his desk. She gazed over the certificates and photos on the walls, the bookcases and cabinets, and scale models of fighter jets.

There was nothing hidden among the papers and files on top of his desk, so she began opening his desk drawers one by one. In the center drawer, she found it: a heavily dogeared and marked-up catalog bearing the name SHURIKAN DEFENSE COMPANY, and below the stylized red throwing star the phrase "Tools, Equipment, and Accessories for the Security-Minded."

She flipped through the pages, bearing in mind the

discussion she'd had with her husband about the kind of weapon that killed Kadeem Nassar.

On page 27 of the catalog, circled several times in blue ink, she saw the sort of thing she was looking for: a combination tactical palm stick and switchblade, which when extended displayed a 2.5-inch serrated steel blade.

She grabbed her phone and snapped a photo.

Chapter 20

The early morning sunlight lit up the faded red brick façade of the central police station as Mason climbed its worn steps, giving it the sort of fresh appearance it must have had when it was unveiled sixty years before.

At the reception window, he said, "I have an appointment with a Lieutenant Raymonde."

It was more than possible the officer behind the glass, seeing his polo shirt and the laptop he was carrying under his arm, assumed he was some sort of IT tech, but the man only asked, "Name?"

"Mason Gates. Or it could be under Gates and Gates Investigations."

"Right," the officer said, after checking a list on a clipboard in front of him. "Head down the hall to your left here. I'll buzz you through into the processing area. Let them know who you're here to see, and they'll escort you up."

In the area beyond the security door, a medium-sized space with rows of hard plastic chairs and a counter with another uniform behind it, he again explained the purpose of his visit, and was led up a flight of stairs to the second floor. The officer took him along to a door about a third of the way down the main corridor, knocked, and poked his head inside.

"Lieutenant, there's a Mr. Gates here to see you."

"Show him in."

It was a small room, with a well-worn desk and two uncomfortable chairs in front of it. A mixture of flyers, memos, personal and work photographs were pinned to the walls, while the back of the room was lined with inexpensive pressed-wood cabinets. The removable nameplate hanging on the office door had said simply LIEUTENANT; the one sitting a few inches from the edge of the desk read LT. STAN RAYMONDE.

The man behind the desk did not look up when Mason entered, but inclined his head toward the intercom on his right.

"Jensen," he said into the box, "we're ready."

Raymonde was a tall man, with a long, craggy face, short gray hair, and a thick salt-and-pepper mustache. The hands flipping through the papers in front of him were long and dexterous; the feet visible beneath the worn metal front of the desk were long and narrow.

Detective Arthur Jensen came in with a notepad in his hand. "Sit down, Gates," he said. "Is that the victim's laptop?"

"As requested," Mason said, and handed it to him.

When the two men were seated, Raymonde folded his hands together and lifted his head. "Nice of you to join us this morning, Mr. Gates," he said with faint irony. "We always appreciate it when the public can make time for us in its busy schedule. I've been given to understand you and we are investigating the same crime."

"From different angles." Mason raised his hands in a conciliatory gesture. "I don't have any intention of getting in your way. Our client simply wants to make sure every possible avenue is being explored in relation to her brother's murder. Given some of the recent cases involving police interactions with minority groups, you can understand her concern."

Raymonde grunted sourly. "I see you remembered to bring the victim's laptop, as Detective Jensen asked you to–what was it, five days ago?"

Mason ignored the implied rebuke and took out his phone.

"This is what we were able to get off of it," he said, scrolling through the menu. "Maybe your people can get more. Around a month and a half ago, around the time he started working on an auditing job for the Canfield Corporation, Kadeem Nassar received the first of three emails from the same address. It was short and to the point:

"'Walk away now. This is not a joke. Leave or you will regret it.'

"Two weeks ago he got a second email, which made the point more strongly: 'Get out now and do not come back. Otherwise you will die, you son of the dog.'"

Detective Jensen grimaced. "Sounds to me like somebody's software did some auto-correcting. But I think we all know what he meant."

Mason nodded.

"Last Wednesday morning Kadeem got another email:

"'This is the final warning. No one wants you here. Quit before it is too late.'

"By that evening, he was dead. It seemed like more than a coincidence to his sister, and I think she's right.

All three emails were sent through a server at Canfield Tower. Now, admittedly, that by itself doesn't prove anything. The killer could simply have been using the free Wi-Fi in the building's lobby. But taken with other facts we've learned, and the incident that happened in front of the building yesterday afternoon…"

"Oh, yes," Raymonde said, "yesterday's incident. We'll get to that in a minute. For now, why don't you tell us what these facts are you've learned, from the beginning."

Mason put his phone away and went into a condensed recital of everything they had so far discovered in the course of their investigations. When he reached his wife's deduction regarding the identity of the CanCorp embezzler, Raymonde narrowed his eyes and nodded.

"You've got a shrewd woman there, Gates. I'd have to agree with her assessment—given the setup you describe, the thief can only be one of the managers in the company's accounting department. But nothing you've told me so far connects that to the Nassar killing in more than a circumstantial way. There's going to have to be a lot more work done before we can say with any certainty the two things are connected, and even more before we have something to present to the district attorney's office. But why am I telling you that? You worked for the DA. You know more than anyone, there's a big step between an investigator's gut instinct and a handful of suspicious facts, and the kind of solid evidence that'll convict in a court of law."

"All too well," Mason replied. "I gave up trying to wrestle with the judicial system, watching guilty people who could afford the fanciest lawyers waltz out of the courtroom while innocent people were railroaded because the best they could get was an overworked public defender, and because the DA's office needed some good press that week... But you didn't ask me here to listen to me give a speech. What about the suspect you mentioned to me, Detective? How did that play out?"

Jensen glanced at his superior, and Raymonde tipped his head briefly in assent.

"When I talked to you on Friday," Jensen said heavily, "we were looking at a con named Scotty Carryll, whose MO fit the killing and who hung around in the same bar as our victim. Carryll hadn't been seen by anyone since Tuesday night, but we had our feelers out. We finally located him–in a lockup in Westfield County. He's been there since the wee hours of Wednesday morning when he was arrested for assault with a deadly weapon after a bar fight in Catersburg. Needless to say, that puts him out of the picture."

"So it's back to the drawing board," Raymonde said. "And word has come down from on high. I'm to take charge of this case personally, to ensure results. That is not a criticism of Detective Jensen, as far as I'm concerned. I have confidence in my investigators. They wouldn't be part of my unit if I didn't think they could do the job. But it seems one of the leading citizens of our great metropolis had a word with the police commissioner about our putting forth a more directed effort. I imagine that was a reaction to having one of the board of directors of his company almost run over in the street yesterday afternoon. Tell me about that, Gates."

Mason did so. Raymonde listened attentively and

then sighed in irritation.

"That's it? That's the critical incident that led to my urgent conference with the brass? A car speeds through an intersection and narrowly misses a couple of ladies in the financial district? That's less conclusive than anything else you've told me. It could've been intentional, sure, but it could just as well have been a drunk driver, or even a preoccupied one, checking his cell phone for the latest stock listings. And the only thing your wife can say for sure is that it was a four-door gray sedan. No license number, no clear description of the driver... However..." Raymonde dropped his head and rifled through the sheets in front of him. "Yes. Something our officers were told during the canvass of Nassar's neighborhood after the murder. A store owner taking his trash out two blocks from the crime scene, around six-fifteen that evening, reported noticing a silvery-gray car parked across the street from his building. He said it was nicer than most of the cars he was used to seeing in his neighborhood, that was why he remembered it; though, like your wife, he couldn't provide any details as to the make and model, and when he finished locking up and left an hour later, the car was no longer there. Not much by itself, but it could indicate a connection between the two incidents."

Mason leaned back in his chair. "Am I allowed to ask if you've come across anything else in your investigation?"

"The only other thing of note so far," Jensen answered, "involves Nassar's credit cards. Someone used them the evening he was killed, purchased an extra-large handful of gift cards at three different stores in Woodlane Mall. It's the smart criminal's way of getting rid of stolen plastic–gift cards are pretty much untraceable."

"Woodlane," Mason said, trying to picture it in his mind. "That's on the east side of town, isn't it?"

"That's right. Just off Upland Boulevard."

"And the clerks at those stores didn't give you any solid descriptions to work with, I assume, or you would've led with that."

Jensen shrugged resignedly and ran his hand across his bald scalp. "What can you do? Typical mall employees. Young people with short attention spans and a keenly-developed lack of interest in the world around them. They couldn't say who bought the cards. They didn't even think it was odd that someone would buy so many cards at once."

"And that brings us up-to-date," Raymonde said. "We all now know how much we don't know. Well, I have no intention of letting the grass grow under our feet. My team is going to reexamine every bit of evidence from the crime scene, including the security tape from Nassar's building. We're going to take a close look at every minute he spent at Canfield Tower over the last two months. In addition, it was strongly intimated to me, Gates, that we're expected to work as closely as possible with your agency until this killer is brought to justice. What that means to me is this: you will notify me the instant you learn of any new evidence bearing on this case. No more five-day delays while you decide what to do with some tip you've gotten or some testimony you've heard. Are we clear?"

"I'm just trying to do the best I can for my client," Mason replied mildly, "and verify all the facts I can relating to Kadeem Nassar's murder before I compile my report."

"Very commendable," Raymonde said drily. "Are we clear?"

Mason rose to his feet and said with a perfectly straight face: "Ten-four, Lieutenant."

Chapter 21

Mason's next step in the investigation, as soon as he got back to his office and looked through the mail that Cecilia had set aside for him, was to reach out to his contact at the DMV and, using the names and addresses his wife had texted to him, compile a list of the vehicles registered to the four accounting managers at CanCorp.

The list was only useful as a starting point. Two of the managers had gray or silver vehicles under their names, but the other two could just as easily have had access to similar-colored sedans belonging to a friend or a neighbor, or simply unlicensed vehicles that they owned themselves.

It was time for legwork.

It made sense to start with the addresses nearer to the office, so he drove north and connected with Archer Avenue, which headed northeast out of the city across the Seaton Milligan Bridge and led him to Holiday Hills on the north side of the river. It was the oldest surviving subdivision in the city, and a large number of the original homes had been replaced by ranch-style structures in the 1960s, which, along with the out-of-date sidewalks and lack of sufficient streetlights, gave it a seedy, middle-class feel.

Matt deWitt lived at 902 Skyline Drive, which had been modernized with waist-high stone veneer and blue siding above that. The driveway in front of the two-car garage was empty, which didn't bode well, but Mason pulled in and rang the doorbell anyway. No response.

He stepped down off the porch and stood at the head of the drive for a moment, letting his gaze sweep across the neighborhood. In either direction along the curving street, a succession of trimmed lawns sloped down to the sidewalk and a series of darkened windows looked out of practically interchangeable houses. After the early morning scurry into work, there was little movement to be seen.

About four houses down on the opposite side of the street, he spotted someone working in the yard. A woman in a flowered hat, a melon-colored blouse and khakis was seated on a wheeled garden seat, planting a row of flowers along the edge of her property.

Mason walked along the sidewalk and called out, "Zinnias?"

She swung her head in his direction. "Dahlias, actually."

"Well, you can tell I'm no gardener," he said, grinning, and stepped into the yard. "They look lovely, either way. I'm sure it takes time to keep a lawn maintained like yours. You're probably out here quite a bit, I'd guess."

"Quite a bit. I even drag my husband into it sometimes, kicking and screaming. What can I do for you?"

Mason came closer and, as he handed her one of his business cards, asked, "Can we keep this between us?"

"I'm the soul of discretion," the woman said with a faint smile, as she took it from him. "Gates and Gates

Investigations," she read. "How d'ye do, Gates and Gates. Sandra Grantham."

"Pleased to meet you," he said, shaking her gloved hand. "I'm looking into an incident involving a gray or silver automobile, and it's possible one of your neighbors might have been involved. Do you know a Mr. deWitt, at number 902?"

She removed her hat briefly and dabbed at her hairline with the back of one glove, revealing a pinned-up mixture of gold and silver strands. "Can't say I particularly do. My husband's spoken to him a few times. They've lived in the neighborhood long enough, though, that we've picked up on a few things about them."

"They?"

"He lives there with his girlfriend, named Madison. Last name Green or Gray or something color-related. They don't have the best of relationships."

"Oh?"

Mrs. Grantham shrugged. "Everyone up and down the street knows it. The number of times they've had shouting matches on the front porch or in the driveway... I always say that's how you can tell people apart–the ones with good breeding have the decency to have their arguments behind closed doors."

Mason's mouth twitched. "I suppose you're right. My records show he drives a gray 2017 Mustang. Does that sound correct?"

"That's what's usually parked in his driveway."

"And his girlfriend? Do you know what kind of car she drives?"

"Something a little older and smaller and pale blue. A Mazda, or maybe an Infiniti? They both have those emblems that look like the letter M to me."

"Would you happen to know if he was home last Wednesday evening around six-thirty? Or let me put it another way–do you remember seeing his car then?"

"I'm afraid I don't particularly. I can mention it to my husband, and have him call you if you want."

"I'd appreciate that. What about yesterday afternoon? Did you happen to notice when he arrived home from work?"

"It was about the same time as usual, I'm sure. He normally gets home around a quarter past four or so."

"He seems like the sort of person who sticks to a regular routine, then?"

"I'd say so. Part of that is his military training, I'm sure–he's in the National Guard. Two weekends a month to defend our country."

Mason couldn't quite decipher the undertone in her words, and took a random guess.

"Your husband was in the military when he was younger, wasn't he?"

"He served in the Army in his twenties, before we were married. Saw action in Grenada and Honduras, and it didn't turn him into a bully who slams doors and screams abuses at women. But there again, it's all in the breeding, isn't it?"

"No doubt."

As he started the engine of his car, Mason was pleased. Mrs. Grantham's information wasn't conclusive by any means. He would need to make another trip out to Holiday Hills, to try and catch deWitt's girlfriend home alone and see what she could add to the picture, and he'd need to let a little time pass before attempting it in order not to tip deWitt off too soon that someone was investigating him.

For a first step, though, it would do nicely.

He drove back into the city, moving south past Winter Avenue to Upland Boulevard, and headed east to Glenn Pines, the subdivision where Mahmud Fathy had his home. It was the last subdivision on that side of the city, before the residential sections gave way to agricultural factories and other industries, and the streets in it were even more winding than those in Holiday Hills. The houses in it felt more secluded as well, since the lots they were on were larger and sprinkled liberally with the spruces and Ponderosa pines that had given the development its name.

Mason was not surprised when no one answered the doorbell of Fathy's residence, which was tucked away toward the rear of the subdivision; it was, after all, midmorning on a weekday. He got back in his car and backed down the driveway to the street, and just as he had in deWitt's neighborhood he took a moment to scan the area for signs of life.

A minute or two later, he spotted an older man walking his dog–along the edge of the street, since there were no sidewalks in the subdivision. Mason climbed out and strolled across to him.

"Excuse me. Do you live nearby?"

"Just around the corner," the man replied. "Are you looking for something?"

"In a manner of speaking," Mason said, and handed him a card. "I'm gathering some information related to an incident involving a silver car. I understand your neighbor here, at 78 Woodlane, may have a car like that."

The man raised the business card at almost arm's

163

length and blinked at it. Mason judged him to be in his sixties; although his bristly mustache was still brown, the thinning hair on his round head was mostly gray. He finished examining the card and returned his gaze to Mason's face as the dog, a Bichon Frise, circled the detective's ankles, sniffing away.

"I left my reading glasses at home," the man said with a self-deprecating chuckle. "Well. I've never met a private eye before. Harold Vintner's my name. And you're… Mr. Gates?" The two shook hands, and he asked, in a lower tone, "Is Mr. Fathy a suspect in some kind of crime?"

"Let's just say I'm gathering some facts for a client and leave it at that."

"Oh. I see. Well, to answer your question, no, Mr. Fathy drives a red sedan."

That description matched the information given to Mason by the DMV, that Mahmud Fathy had one vehicle registered to his name, a cherry-red 2014 Chevrolet SS. But he had to look under every stone nonetheless.

"Do you know him very well?"

"Not really," Vintner answered. "I know he has some sort of job downtown, in the financial sector. But he keeps to himself mostly. I imagine that could be at least partly because he doesn't speak English very well. He wasn't born here, you know."

"Oh, no?"

Vintner nodded. "Somewhere in the Middle East, I'm not sure exactly where."

"Does he live alone?"

"All by himself. He could be a widower for all I know, he's never said."

"And you've never seen a gray or silver car in his driveway?"

"Actually, now that you mention it, his cousin drives a silver four-door, and he comes to visit on occasion. I've talked to him once or twice. His name's Abdul or Abdullah, something like that. He's in real estate. I have his card in a drawer somewhere at home."

"You said you live around the corner. You probably don't have a good view of his driveway from your house, then?"

"Not really. I can just see the east side of his house through the trees from my back porch. But I do pass this way three or four times a day." Vintner gazed down fondly at the animal on the end of his leash. "Our little Maximilian's bladder just doesn't hold up the way it used to. Neither, between you and me, does mine, so I can't hold it against him. At any rate, we go for walksies several times between breakfast and bedtime. I was right–you are looking for something in particular, aren't you?"

"Would you happen to have strolled past last Wednesday evening, around six-thirty or so? I assume Mr. Fathy is normally home by that time?"

"Yes, he gets home in the late afternoon, generally. But I can't say I distinctly remember last Wednesday, and I'm not sure it would help you if I did. He parks his car in the garage, so I wouldn't know if he was home then or not. That is what you're wanting to know, isn't it?"

"It might have helped. Thank you, Mr. Vintner. If you happen to find his cousin's card, the one in real estate, could you give me a call? I'd like to get his phone number."

"Can do," the man said, and with a cheery wave, he and Maximilian toddled away down the street. Mason sighed and climbed into his car.

Chapter 22

When noon rolled around, Amirah insisted that Janeen Walkowitz have lunch with her. She wasn't taking any chances on something happening to the woman while she was out of her sight, whether that was in her office or at a crowded restaurant–although Amirah wasn't entirely sure what she could do if the killer decided to strike again.

Jerald Canfield, after the previous day's incident, had given instructions for building security to accompany Ms. Walkowitz to and from the employee garage, but even so, Amirah found her nerves on edge as the three of them rode the elevator down to the lobby. She told herself she was being ridiculous: it was true that they were hanging helplessly in midair in a glass cage, but the only things across from them were the massive panels of the front of the building. Unless the killer was some sort of human fly super-sniper, they would be fine at least until they stepped through the lobby doors.

They made it to her car without incident, and Amirah drove them across town to the agency. Mason had agreed to make it a working lunch. Cecilia had ordered from the Chinese restaurant at the far end of the strip mall, and the four of them ate at the little conference table in the back room, hot and sour soup and dim sum and General Tso's chicken.

"So," Amirah announced, juggling her chopsticks, "we have four suspects. How about we go through the list one at a time and see where we're at?"

"Before we start," her husband asked, "can we eliminate anyone based on when the embezzling started? That was eight years ago, I think you told me. Did any of the four accounting managers join the company after that point?"

Ms. Walkowitz shook her head. "No, that doesn't help us. All four of them have been with my department at least that long."

"Unusual in this day and age," murmured Mason.

"We offer very attractive benefits," she replied with quiet pride.

"Okay. Here we go." Amirah popped a dumpling in her mouth and talked around it. "The North manager, Samantha Atchison. She's around our age, very pleasant, very accommodating."

"She started in Accounting eight years ago," added Ms. Walkowitz.

"Oh-oh," said Cecilia.

Mason smiled at her. "We won't jump to any conclusions just yet."

"More than anything else," Amirah said, "she makes me think of a bunny."

Mason brought his eyebrows together quizzically. "A Playboy Bunny?"

"No, no," Amirah laughed, "an actual bunny– although she does have nice long legs, the kind I wouldn't mind having. She has this pink-and-white complexion and big blue eyes, and just seems sweet and cuddly. She insists that everyone call her 'Sammi.' Who knows? Maybe she's really super-competitive deep down inside."

"She does drive a silver car, according to the license bureau, but I haven't had a chance to check up on her movements yet."

"Right. Then the West manager, Matt deWitt. I only met him briefly the other day. I'd say he's about thirty, has a military-style haircut, seemed very businesslike."

"He's in the National Guard," Ms. Walkowitz said, confirming what Mason had been told, "which I imagine accounts for his demeanor. He's very good with numbers, though. He's been with us around ten years, I think."

"He has the right kind of car as well," Mason said. "He could stand some more looking into."

"I found a self-defense catalog in his office," said Amirah, "and he had a weapon circled that sounded a lot like the one that was used on Kadeem Nassar." She pulled out her phone and showed them the photo she had taken of the palmstick-switchblade.

"We'd have to prove he actually ordered the item," her husband mused, "and that he still had it at the time of the murder…"

"The Southeast manager, Gerome Westbrook," Amirah continued, "is in his mid-forties, I'd say. He's slender and brown-haired and comes from a wealthy family; his father golfs with the company CEO, a Mr. Nederostek. There's something going on with him, though. He looked to me like he's under some kind of strain."

"I don't know the details," said Ms. Walkowitz, "but there's some sort of crisis taking place in his life. In the last eight months, he's used up just about every bit of personal and vacation time he had accrued. But I find it hard to believe he could be stealing from the company. He's worked at CanCorp for more than twenty years... Not that I can honestly believe any of my managers is a thief."

"And a killer," supplied Amirah. "But facts are facts. It has to be one of the four."

"If this Westbrook is the one," asked Cecilia, "would he really have waited years before starting his embezzling?"

Mason shrugged. "Could be any number of explanations for that. Maybe he only figured out how to steal the money eight years ago. Or maybe the phony account Amirah and Sa'id discovered isn't the first one he set up. It would be the smart thing to do, to close out the fake account every so often and open up a new one that didn't have any obvious connection to it."

Amirah asked Ms. Walkowitz, "Does Mr. Westbrook have any medical or military background? Anything that might've given him a knowledge of anatomy?"

The older woman shook her head. "Not that I'm aware of."

"According to the DMV," Mason said, "he drives an SUV, not a sedan, but there is a second vehicle, registered primarily under his wife's name. I'll follow up on that this afternoon."

"Lastly, then, we have the Southwest manager, Mahmud Fathy. I met him briefly on Monday as well. He's in his fifties, and wasn't born here in the US, so he doesn't speak English fluently. I've been told he stays in his office most of the time and communicates with his team by email."

"He joined the company nine years ago," Ms. Walkowitz said, "just after he came to this country. He was in the Quartermaster Corps of the Egyptian Army previously, so he had plenty of experience at handling funds."

"If he's from the Middle East himself," Cecilia murmured, "it doesn't seem likely he'd write 'Die Arab' on someone's car."

"He doesn't drive the right kind of car, either," Mason said, "but he has a cousin who does. He could have arranged to borrow his cousin's car to carry out these attacks."

"So," Amirah asked brightly of the group, "any thoughts?"

"I'd say this Matt deWitt sounds like the most plausible candidate," her husband answered, "but there's plenty of work to be done yet before we reach any verdicts."

"Any more news on the accounting front?" Amirah asked Ms. Walkowitz.

The older woman swallowed a mouthful of rice and vegetables before replying. "Yes. It took most of the morning, but we learned what 'BDFN' stands for on the dummy account withdrawals. Banco de Finanzas in Nicaragua, and specifically the main branch in Managua. In other words, what's commonly known as an 'off-shore' banking location. I spoke to someone at the national police headquarters there, and they agreed to look into the matter and get back to us. I don't expect any quick results, though."

With that, lunch was over. When Amirah and Ms. Walkowitz arrived back at the accounting head's office downtown they found a pastel Post-It stuck to the older woman's computer screen. It read simply: Call Detective Jensen. 799-605-1783

She showed the note to Amirah, who shrugged, to let her know she knew nothing about it.

Ms. Walkowitz settled into the chair behind her desk and dialed.

"Put him on speaker," Amirah whispered, perching on the edge of the desk.

The auditor, George, glanced up from his folding table briefly and returned to his work.

The phone buzzed twice and then the opposite party picked up. "Detective Jensen here."

"Janeen Walkowitz, from CanCorp. I have a note that you wanted me to call you?"

"Yes. Thank you, Ms. Walkowitz. I left you a voicemail, but it was imperative for me to reach you as soon as possible, so I also had someone from your staff leave a message. Our department is moving forward in the investigation of Kadeem Nassar's death, and we need to begin preliminary interviews with the members of your accounting division. Starting with you first, if you don't mind. I'd like to start the interviews first thing tomorrow morning, if that can be arranged."

"I'm sure it can."

"Good. I think everyone involved would prefer we do this at your building, so I'll need a room set aside where I can speak to people one-on-one–it doesn't have to be a large one. And it would be helpful if your management team could all be there in the morning. You have four accounting managers, is that right?"

"Yes, that's right. I'll see what I can do, Detective. I'm sure we can get something set up for you."

"I appreciate it, Ms. Walkowitz. I'll see you

tomorrow."

The accounting head pressed the power button on the phone set and turned to Amirah with a faint wondering expression.

Amirah seemed to realize she was sitting on the woman's desk and hopped to her feet. "Will you have any problem setting up a room for him?" she asked.

"No, there's a small conference room at the end of the main corridor that doesn't get used much. He's welcome to use that."

Amirah bit her lip and managed to look thoughtful and a little mischievous at the same time. "Is there any way I might be able to listen in on his interviews without his knowing?"

Ms. Walkowitz scrunched her mouth up and faint lines appeared between her eyebrows. "I'm not sure about the legality of that. If any of the employees found out someone was eavesdropping on their conversations…"

"They aren't exactly privileged exchanges, though, if they're being questioned by the police. And don't the conference rooms all have security cameras in them already?"

"Yes, but they're video only. There's no sound."

"That's all right. At least we're halfway there. Just let me work on it."

For the rest of the afternoon, Amirah sat in with the West accounting unit, Matt deWitt's team. DeWitt shook Amirah's hand firmly but let go of it quickly when Ms. Walkowitz brought her to his office, and his comment on the arrangement was terse.

"Good to have you."

The West team had three accountants: Anita, a

mother of two, with dark hair in a pixie cut and glasses that she kept pushing onto the top of her head; Enrique, middle-aged and Hispanic, wearing a tweed jacket with elbow patches; and Steph, who had her light brown hair pinned up and whose broad-striped sweater appeared handmade. Amirah, intending to ease into her questions about the managers, found to her surprise that the rumor mill in the building had been at work, and the three of them were full of their own questions, about the incident in the crosswalk the previous afternoon.

"Is it true, you and Ms. Walkowitz were almost run over?"

"What exactly happened?"

"Did you have any suspicion the driver wasn't going to stop?"

Amirah held her hands up in surrender and gave the three a basic summary of their narrow escape from the speeding car, doing her best to make it sound as if the episode was completely unexpected.

"I hope that sort of thing doesn't happen much around here!" she concluded with a faint laugh. "If I'm going to have to race across the street to get to my car safely, I'll have to start wearing more sensible shoes."

Enrique shook his head. "Traffic can get crazy sometimes during the day, but I've never seen anything like that. Some people just should never be allowed behind the wheel."

"No doubt," Amirah said. "I suppose chances are really pretty slim it could happen again. But how about inside Canfield Tower? You've never had any workplace incidents I should be worried about, have you?"

"You mean like someone bringing a gun into the

building?" asked Anita. "We haven't had anything like that as long as I've been here, and besides, we have security in the lobby. They'd lock the building down immediately if something like that happened."

"And the employees get along all right?" Amirah responded. "They don't get into fights in the break room or arguments in the halls?"

"Not that I've ever heard," Steph said. "This is a white-collar environment. People here are more likely to post mean comments on each other's Facebook pages than confront each other in person."

"What's the work environment like? The employees don't have any issues with management, do they?"

"Not in our department, at least."

"How's Mr. deWitt to work for? I shadowed Ms. Atchison's team this morning…"

"He doesn't say much," Anita answered, "but I don't think he's a bad boss. He just takes his job very seriously and expects his employees to do the same."

"Have you ever seen him lose his temper?"

The three shook their heads in unison.

"I understand he's a military guy," Amirah said. "Someone told me earlier he likes to bring in catalogs from some self-defense company and share them."

Enrique chuckled. "Oh, yeah. His catalogs. That's probably the only thing I've seen him get really enthusiastic about. Can't say I blame him, though. That place he shops with carries a lot of interesting stuff–not just weapons, but coffee mugs, keychains, T-shirts, you name it."

"He's talked a lot of us into buying things from it," said Anita. "I have an emergency whistle on my keychain I got from there. Thankfully I've never had to use it."

"As much as he loves those catalogs," Enrique added, "it was actually Mr. Fathy that introduced him to them. I guess he bought something from the company when he first came to this country, and when he found out Mr. deWitt was in the National Guard, he gave him their catalog."

"Mr. Fathy? One of the other managers?"

"That's right."

"What are the other managers like? Is there a certain team I should try to get on?"

"Ms. Atchison seems good-natured," Steph said, "but it isn't like we deal with the other managers much. We sometimes talk to them just in passing, or at one of the company parties, but that's about it. Mr. Westbrook looks like he's got a lot on his mind lately. Maybe his team isn't doing so well at meeting their goals. Mr. Fathy–well, who knows?"

"What she means," clarified Anita, "is that Mr. Fathy hides out in his office all day, and says hardly anything to anybody. His English isn't good, and I suppose he's self-conscious about it."

"I've been told he communicates with his team mostly by email," Amirah said.

"Exactly," said Enrique. "He has some kind of software to translate whatever he types into English, to make it easier for him. But even then it sometimes comes out a little unclear."

"That's interesting. I've also heard rumors there's some kind of company audit going on. Have any of you met the auditor? Should I be concerned about that?"

The three shook their heads.

"There've been two auditors now," confided Steph in a low voice. "The first one was a young guy who got killed in some kind of robbery. It was on the news this past weekend. The second's an older guy, black, but I've never talked to him. Whoever they are, and whatever company they're from, they work with Ms. Walkowitz–our big chief, the Director of Accounting– and only with her. The rest of us just aren't in the loop."

Enrique shrugged. "Companies like this one have to be audited from time to time. It's just part of the process. The way I look at it, as long as we're all still getting a paycheck there can't be anything to worry about, right?"

From there the conversation drifted to other topics. The members of the West team seemed not to know anything else that could be relevant to Amirah's investigation, and as the afternoon wore on she found herself taking little in the way of notes, and struggling to keep her eyes open.

She hadn't said anything to her husband, or to Ms. Walkowitz, but she hadn't slept well the night before. The previous day's events had caught up with her in the dark, and her dreams were full of large vehicles, the size of Humvees or bigger, that she was struggling to outrun–and of course, she was in stiletto heels, which kept catching in the mud and slowing her down. She woke up in a sweat at one point to find Mason sleeping like a baby, with his mouth hanging open. She glared at him, for all the good that did, and lay there for more than an hour, staring at the ceiling, before dozing off again.

By the end of their workday, as she ferried Janeen Walkowitz through the late afternoon traffic, Amirah was left with the feeling that she hadn't accomplished much of anything. It wasn't until later, after she had deposited the accounting head safely at the door of her Midcentury-modern home and was driving back to the agency's offices, that certain things she'd been told clicked together in her head, and she knew–or at least had a very strong suspicion–who had killed Kadeem Nassar.

Chapter 23

For his part, Mason Gates drove to the southwest corner of the city after lunch was over, to Falshire West, the subdivision where Samantha Atchison lived.

As soon as he came into sight of the entrance to the neighborhood he knew he was going to have trouble. Falshire West was a gated community, encircled by a wall of dull sand-colored stones and wrought iron, with cameras posted at regular intervals. A guard in a dark gray uniform sat in the gatehouse, flipping unenthusiastically through a magazine.

Mason turned off Falls Parkway and onto the gateway apron in a wide swing, positioning his car half on the concrete and half on the grass to not block the entrance. He walked over to the guardhouse and got exactly the reception he was expecting.

The guard frowned at him. "Can I help you? You can't park there, you know."

Mason took out his wallet and held it up so the man could see his investigator's license, thinking that might make the strongest impression on him. "I was hoping to pay a visit to one of the residents, to answer some questions relating to an ongoing case."

"Address?"

"38 Butternut Court. A Ms. Samantha Atchison."

The guard glanced at a clipboard in front of him. "I don't have anything down here, and I can't let anyone inside without specific authorization from one of the homeowners. Besides," the young man added with a faint laugh, "you wouldn't catch anybody at home there now, anyway."

"It sounds like you know Ms. Atchison pretty well."

The guard realized he had possibly said too much and muttered, "Maybe."

"I hear she's a nice lady."

"Sure."

Mason put on his best "just-between-us" manner.

"Well then, maybe you'd like to do her a favor. I'm not here to get her in trouble. The case I'm on involves an incident at the company where she works, and we just need to eliminate some names from our list of the people concerned, so we know they had nothing to do with it. You might be able to tell me what I need to know, and in that case I'll never have to bother her."

The guard looked uncertain. "I don't think I should answer any questions. I could get in real hot water sharing personal information about the residents."

"Why don't I let you decide for yourself?" Mason said, and went on before he could get an objection. "For instance, the information I have is that she drives a silver Hyundai Genesis. Does that sound right?"

"Yeah, that's right."

"You see? You didn't give away anything confidential. Do you know if she owns any other vehicles?"

"No, that's it."

"And no one else at her residence owns a vehicle?"

"There isn't anyone else. Anyone else old enough to drive, I mean. It's just her and her two boys, and the oldest one only just turned fifteen."

"Oh?" Mason asked casually. "She doesn't have a husband, or a boyfriend, or…?"

The guard said quickly, "No, she doesn't."

Mason eyed him speculatively and added, "Really? An attractive woman like that isn't seeing anybody?"

The young man stared out across the parkway, breathing through his nose while he moved his lips in a silent struggle, and then he looked Mason in the eyes and blurted:

"She has a lot on her plate right now. She's divorced, a single mother, and she's focusing on taking care of her kids. She goes to work, and she takes the boys to their after-school activities, and that's it."

Mason said quietly, "It can't be easy, juggling everything like that."

"No. And you'd better believe it isn't cheap, living in a place like this, but it's what's best for them. She had an abusive husband. Even after the divorce he stalked her and threatened her. She had to move them in here and cut off contact with everyone she knew, even her own family except for her sister, so she could be sure he couldn't get to them. She was barely making ends meet when they first got here, working two jobs and putting herself through night school to learn accounting, but they needed to be someplace safe. She even started taking self-defense classes in case her ex caught up with her again."

Mason surveyed the young man's earnest, moon-shaped face and buzzcut blond hair and thought that he must have had quite a few conversations with Ms. Atchison to know that much about her–and that he very likely had the desire to be more than an employee to her.

He also thought that a couple million dollars would allow Ms. Atchison to put a lot more distance between her and her abusive ex-husband.

"I only have one or two more questions," he said. "Maybe you could help me out with those, too. No reason to add to Ms. Atchison's worries."

The guard puffed through his nose again, but he'd already committed himself.

"I don't know what else I can tell you."

"Do you keep any kind of log here at the gate, of who goes in and goes out?"

"Yeah, it registers in the system every time the residents use their keycard, and I have to make an entry whenever I buzz a visitor in or out."

"Good. Could you tell me if Ms. Atchison got home around the usual time yesterday? I'm assuming it would have been between four-fifteen and four-thirty."

The guard tapped at his antiquated keyboard, and a line of green figures scrolled up the small black screen of the monitor.

"Yeah, scanned in at four-eighteen yesterday."

Mason frowned. "What about last Wednesday? Any way of telling if she was home around six-thirty that evening?"

The guard sighed and plugged away at his keyboard some more. "Wednesday, was it? I can tell you where she was then without looking. She takes her youngest to softball practice twice a week, Wednesdays and Fridays... See, I was right. She left here at five-forty-one, didn't get back until eight-thirty-five."

Mason smiled. "Thank you. That's all. You see— we took care of that without having to disturb a single one of your homeowners."

As he drove away Mason mulled over the times he'd been given. If Samantha Atchison had reached home at 4:18 the previous day it seemed unlikely she could have been driving the car that almost ran his wife over, given that Amirah figured the incident happened between four-twenty and four-thirty; on the other hand, the woman could easily have slipped away from her son's softball practice the previous Wednesday long enough to kill Kadeem Nassar.

From Falls Parkway he took the Route 44 connection east, to the home of the last of the four suspects, Gerome Westbrook. Of the four account managers, Westbrook was the only one who didn't live in some sort of subdivision. Instead, he resided in a large, stately Federal-style house in a quiet, dignified neighborhood, where any ruffians were most likely to be college boys on a weekend bender.

There were no cars in the driveway, which he took to be a sign that no one would be home, but when he rang the doorbell the front door was opened by a dark-haired woman with a hard expression and heavy circles under her eyes.

"Mrs. Westbrook?"

"Ms. Carlsberg. Can I help you?"

He showed her his investigator's license. "I'm investigating an incident involving a silver vehicle, and the name Gerome Westbrook came up in connection with it. Is there someone here who might be able to answer a few questions for me? This is his address, isn't it?"

"Gerome doesn't have a silver vehicle. He drives a tan SUV. Is that all?"

That was the information Mason had gotten from the BMV, that Gerome Westbrook owned a bronze 2013 Ford Escape, but there had also been a second automobile registered to his name and address.

"He doesn't own anything else?" Mason prodded.

The woman crossed her arms and glared at him. "There's my sister's Lexus, but it hasn't been out of the garage in months."

"And your sister is…?"

"Fay Westbrook. Gerome's wife. Trust me, she hasn't been driving it. Now if that's everything–"

Mason almost had the urge to stick his foot in the door, suspecting the woman was about to slam it on him. He said quickly, "I realize you weren't expecting my visit, but I promise you, I only have one or two more questions, and then I'll leave. You said the Lexus hadn't been driven in months. Are you certain of that, and can you describe the car for me?"

Ms. Carlsberg's eyes blazed. She stepped forward onto the porch suddenly, yanking the door shut behind her but cushioning it so it closed quietly. Mason, caught off guard, moved quickly back out of her way.

"You listen to me, and you listen good! I'm going to say this once"—she thrust her forefinger in the air in front of his nose– "one time, and then you can get off this property. Gerome bought that car, a mint-green Lexus ES, for Fay eight months ago, as an anniversary present. She got to enjoy it for just three weeks before the doctors told her her cancer was back. My sister has stage 4 pancreatic adenocarcinoma. She's dying. So I don't care who you are or who you're working for, you can take your questions and shove them!"

There were times as a cop when Mason had felt

like a heel, aware he was only adding to a grieving family's pain by insisting on having his questions answered while they were trying to process the death of a loved one. He had that same feeling now, and the excuse that he had a job to do was still just as lousy.

"I am so sorry," he said. "I wouldn't have dreamed of intruding on you like this if I'd had the slightest idea. Is there any chance her cancer might go into remission?"

"Maybe," Ms. Carlsberg gritted, hugging her arms over her chest and gazing off into the distance. "A very small chance. The doctors suggested trying to get her in to Cedars-Sinai or the Mayo Clinic for a new, experimental treatment, but the treatment's very expensive and very aggressive. They would've had to sell the house and just about everything else, and Carley, their daughter, would've had to give up college. Even then it might only give her a few more years, and her quality of life…"

Mason waited for a moment while the woman regained her composure, then said, "Please, just bear with me a little longer, and I won't bother you anymore. Do you happen to know where Mr. Westbrook was last Wednesday around six-thirty p.m.?"

"Yes, he was here with us, having dinner."

"And what time did he get home from work yesterday?"

"His normal time, about four-twenty or so, as far as I know."

There was some room for doubt with that last reply, but Mason let it go. He apologized again and made his way back to the agency with a heavy heart and churning thoughts.

Could the motive for the embezzling be more than simple greed? He would have to look into when Mrs. Westbrook's cancer was originally diagnosed. It was narrowly possible her husband could have taken his wife's car the previous day without anyone else in the household being aware of it, but he apparently had a solid alibi for the time Kadeem Nassar was killed.

So far, as Mason had told his wife earlier, Matt deWitt appeared to be their most likely suspect.

He was still idly thinking about the various neighborhoods he had been to that day when he stepped over the threshold of his office, and as he did a thought struck him, something he remembered from his conversation with the police and should have remembered sooner. He sat down at his desk and pulled up a map of the city on his computer.

Sure enough, once he located the four addresses on the screen, he had a pretty reasonable idea who had killed Kadeem Nassar.

Chapter 24

When Amirah reached the agency and entered her husband's office, the first thing she said was, "I'm worried."

Mason, who was on hold with the police department, looked up at her and raised his eyebrows in interrogation.

"I just realized, my sister Aziza hasn't called once today about the anniversary party for *baba* and *mum*," she explained, dropping into the chair next to his desk. "I can only imagine what over-the-top idea she's cooking up now. Whatcha doing?"

He grinned at her but before he could answer someone came on the other end of the line, and he said, "Hello?"

"Gates? This is Detective Jensen."

"Oh, Jensen. I was trying to reach Lieutenant Raymonde, but you'll do."

"Thanks," Jensen replied drily. "Good to know. The lieutenant's a little busy to be taking random phone calls throughout the day. You got something for us on this Nassar killing?"

"Just an idea that struck me, and I wanted to run it by you. When I was there this morning you told me how Kadeem's credit cards were used at Woodlane Mall after he was killed. It occurred to me his killer might also have disposed of the black hoodie he wore at the same mall."

"Yeah. We thought of that two days ago. No luck. If the killer did leave it there somewhere, it's either buried at the city dump by now or someone took it home and washed all the evidence out of it."

"I can see you're not sitting on your hands," Mason said. "Well, in the interest of cooperation, is there a direct email where I can send you any other facts or possibilities we run across?"

"Sure. Why not?" Jensen responded sourly. "Send me a message the next time you have a brainwave. I can always spare a few minutes to read about leads we've already thought of. It'll just brighten up my day."

Mason rolled his eyes but with persistence managed to get Jensen's work email.

Amirah, who could hear pretty much the whole conversation from where she was sitting, scrunched up her face at her husband as he hit the disconnect button. "Poor baby. But never mind him. I have some news that'll cheer you up. I think I know who killed Kadeem Nassar."

He smiled. "So do I. But let's hear your theory first."

Amirah explained to him the points she had pieced together earlier. "…It's the special software he uses," she concluded. "That's why the second email was worded the way it was."

Mason nodded and turned his computer monitor toward her to show her the opened map of the city. "And the subdivision where he lives, right here, borders on Woodlane Mall, where Nassar's credit cards were used after the murder. There's even a back way into the mall that connects directly to his street."

"There's no doubt of it, then. We've got him."

"We have something. The fact we both came up with the same name tells me we're on the right track, but, honey, so far everything we have is circumstantial. There's nothing in the way of direct evidence linking him with the murder."

"Then what do we do?" she asked.

"We'll do what we told Leila Nassar we'd do for her. We'll draw up a full report for her covering every aspect of the case, as well as forwarding a copy to Detective Jensen, and she can take it from there. Hopefully, the police will listen to her and make our suspect their primary suspect. Otherwise, in a year or two, we'll be into the second phase of our work for her, digging into his activities for her attorney in the civil trial."

Amirah frowned thoughtfully. Mason, who recognized the signs that she was in the process of making up her mind about something, waited with some apprehension for what she would say next.

"We don't have proof yet," she said finally, "but we may by tomorrow. Detective Jensen is going to be interviewing the accounting managers tomorrow morning. If I listen in on his interviews I may catch something that connects with what we already know, and then…"

"How exactly do you figure on doing that, sugar plum? Not to crush your hopes, but I don't believe Jensen will be inviting you to sit in."

Amirah made a face at him and took a set of small objects from her purse, two plastic squares roughly three inches by three inches and an abbreviated earpiece.

"I was halfway here when the idea struck me, and I doubled back to my cousin Sa'id's to get these. I remembered the two of you discussing surveillance equipment a while back, and I was sure he'd still have some samples in his workshop. This is a wireless microphone/transmitter and receiver, with a Bluetooth earpiece. Good up to two hundred feet, which should be plenty enough for what I need them for. Battery-powered, so all I need to do is slip the transmitter into a corner of the interview room, and I can listen in on everything."

Mason was frowning, and Amirah went on quickly to cut off his potential objections.

"I know. I know we told Leila the most we could do for her was to compile a report with the evidence we found, but I don't want to leave it at that. Sweetheart, this man killed her brother just because Kadeem was good at his job, just for the sake of a lot of money. Not to mention attempting to add Janeen Walkowitz and me to that list. I don't want to give him a chance to get away, or to hurt anyone else."

"Something tells me," Mason said, "you have more in mind than you've mentioned so far."

Amirah nodded determinedly. "I want to nail him, once and for all."

"Meaning…?" he prodded patiently.

"If the surveillance doesn't come up with anything, if we're still where we are now by noon tomorrow, I think we should set a trap for him."

"A trap, hmm? Just what do you have in mind?"

She described the idea she had. Mason leaned back in his chair.

"We'd have to get a prop or two from Ms. Nassar

to make it work," he said, "and we'd have to get the upper management at CanCorp to agree... But be aware, there's always the possibility that it won't work. Then we'd only have put the killer on his guard, and given him the incentive to slip away before the police find some conclusive evidence."

"Well, we'll deal with that when it happens. But we have to at least try, don't we?"

"I can't argue with that sentiment, can I? Since I now have Detective Jensen's email, I'll send him a brief outline of all the facts we've got so far. Maybe he can use them to his advantage in his interviews tomorrow. If that doesn't pan out, then we'll try your suggestion, and go to Plan B."

Amirah grinned, threw her arms around her husband's neck, and kissed him soundly on the mouth.

Chapter 25

After that Amirah went into the back room for a nap, and Mason headed out to tackle his last task for the afternoon, a somewhat desperate attempt to wrap up the Supreme Insurance fraud case. They had been working on that case for two weeks now, which was not particularly unusual–insurance cases generally took around a month to resolve–but their persistent bad luck with it was beginning to get on his nerves.

Mason's strategy this time was a solo effort. He'd determined which cable company Richard Daniel Reeves and Amal Wright subscribed to, and he stopped first at the business's back offices, where he persuaded one of the employees to rent him a company polo and ball cap for twenty-four hours and provide him with some random blank paperwork. Armed with these articles and a clipboard, he rang the doorbell at 1746B Bayberry Street.

Reeves opened the door and looked him up and down. Today his extra-large T-shirt proclaimed allegiance to Radiohead.

"Yeah?" he asked.

Mason went into the act he had prepared, hoping the young man hadn't gotten a good look at him from the last time he had been on that porch, rescuing his partner from an irate woman with a broom.

"Richard Reeves?"

"Yeah?"

"Sorry to bother you," Mason said, "but our company's received notification of some service fluctuations in the neighborhood. We're examining the inside connections at the houses of our customers, to see if we can pinpoint the cause. All right with you if I come inside to run a check?"

"Sure, why not?"

Mason's idea was to gain entry into the house and poke around for a little bit, hoping that Reeves would let his guard down in front of the "cable guy" and act in some way that demonstrated he was faking his injuries. The next part, however, was the crucial bit.

"I'll need to video the work I do," he added, holding up his phone. "Do I have your permission to film inside your house?"

"Knock yourself out."

"Okay. Sign here, and initial here."

The only way any video or audio recording would be admissible in court would be if he got the subject's permission to record, or the permission of the owner of whatever building he happened to be in at the time. Now, having signed the piece of paper Mason had presented him–even though the paperwork itself was meaningless–Reeves had no way of contesting whatever Mason happened to film inside.

Mason followed him into the living room, where a 64-inch flat-screen TV took up all of one corner. Reeves' roommate was sitting on the futon opposite it. Amal Wright was slender, especially in comparison to Reeves, with skin a couple shades darker than caramel, and was wearing a gray tank top and knee-length Nike shorts.

Mason had not actually figured out what exactly he would do once he was inside the apartment. He had brought along a small voltage tester from a tool kit he kept at the office, and was intending to point it at various connections in the vicinity of the television while keeping his phone subtly turned toward Reeves to capture any questionable movements.

Reeves eased himself down onto the other side of the futon. Mason had the roommate, Wright, flip through the channels once or twice with the remote, and then got down on his knees to reach behind the TV to the wall jack, holding his phone in his outside hand so that it was angled in their direction.

A moment or two later he heard:

*"You know who that is, don't you?"*

*"Who? The cable guy?"*

Mason stiffened at the unexpected exchange, and had to force himself to act as if he hadn't heard anything.

They were speaking Arabic.

It was one of those odd coincidences in life, where no amount of foreknowledge could have predicted how events and circumstances would combine. The two roommates were no doubt positive there was no chance this random Caucasian man would understand them, not having any idea he was the one private investigator in the city who was married to an Arab-American woman. And how was it that they spoke Arabic? Was Wright, who was apparently mixed-race, the son of an Arab-American? Mason turned his phone slightly more towards them and tilted it up a little, to be sure they were squarely in the center of the picture.

*"He doesn't work for the cable company,"* Reeves

explained to his companion. *"He's a private dick, one of the two that were here the other day. You remember? Old lady Horvath whaled on his buddy with a broom?"*

*"Oh, yeah. They tried to get you with that fake delivery."*

*"Right. Like I was going to fall for that. I've been dealing with these insurance guys long enough I know better. Some package just shows up on my door, no email delivery confirmation, and I'm just going to bend down and pick it up? I don't think so."*

*"So what are you going to do?"*

*"Nothing. Let him poke around the apartment, pretending to work for the cable company, if he wants. He's not going to catch me out. I fooled the insurance companies before, I can fool this joker too."*

*"We just let him fiddle around with the TV?"*

*"For as long as he wants. Why not? I'll be laughing my way to the bank when this is over."*

Well, Mason thought as he rose from the floor, someone would be laughing, at any rate.

Chapter 26

Detective Arthur Jensen arrived on the forty-first floor of Canfield Tower at 8 a.m. exactly the next morning, to begin his interviews with the accounting department. That gave Amirah Gates plenty of time to place her transmitter unobtrusively in a corner of the small room that had been set aside for his use.

As he had declared over the phone, he began by questioning Janeen Walkowitz, which took nearly forty-five minutes. Upon emerging from the interview room, before summoning the next person on the detective's list, Ms. Walkowitz poked her head into her office and gave a quick signal to Amirah, who was waiting in one corner. This was the younger woman's cue to hurry to the elevators and down one floor to the company's IT department, where she'd be able to view the feed from the security camera.

She headed for the workbench of the employee she'd been introduced to the previous afternoon, a pudgy young man with a thin mustache whom everyone called Hershey (short for Herschel, which he refused to answer to). He had an auxiliary laptop and extra chair set up for her and the feed from the interview room camera was already running on the screen. As Ms. Walkowitz had explained, there was no sound along with the image, so Amirah was the only one who would be able to hear what was being said.

She switched on the receiver she had brought with her, setting it down next to the laptop, and slipped the earpiece into her ear. Hershey, after staring at her for a few seconds, turned away and resumed working on his computer.

Jensen was beginning his interview with the North manager, Samantha Atchison, his bald head gleaming in the overhead lighting. The manager was dressed in a dark skirt that was short but not unprofessional, with a long-sleeved blouse in wide stripes of white and pale rose, and her frizzy blond hair was pulled to the back of her head in a single cascade.

Amirah had spoken to the four managers here and there, enough to get a general impression of each of their personalities, but this was her first opportunity to observe them at length. Ms. Atchison's usual cheerful demeanor seemed subdued this morning. She kept clasping her arms across her chest and then unclasping them, as if unable to relax.

"...And our information seems to indicate Mr. Nassar was killed by someone associated with CanCorp," Jensen explained. "I understand you met with him when he began working on the company audit?"

"Yes, briefly. That's right."

"How did he strike you? That is, how would you describe his personality? Was he abrasive, the sort to step on toes, or did he keep to himself?"

Ms. Atchison gave a short laugh. "You're asking a lot of me, aren't you? I only had a short conversation with him that first day, not enough to really tell anything about him. He seemed professional enough."

"Did you interact much with him as time went on?"

"No, not at all."

It was hard to tell whether Jensen had had the time to read Mason Gates' explanatory email before beginning these interviews or not. His questions were tentative and apparently unconsidered; it was likely he was on a fishing expedition at this point, to see what indications he could gather before the police settled on an official suspect.

Amirah, for her part, was waiting for any clue or comment that would confirm the guilt of the person she and her husband had named. It was quickly beginning to feel as if she would be waiting for a while.

"Did you hear any rumors or remarks," Jensen asked, "about him having a confrontation with any CanCorp employees? I have a note here about an argument in the elevator…"

"Was that him? I remember hearing about that, but I didn't know who was involved, just that a manager from another department got into it with someone. You think that had something to do with his being killed?"

"Anything's possible, isn't it? What about after work? Did you ever run into him outside office hours?"

Ms. Atchison widened her blue eyes. "What do you mean?"

"It isn't unheard of for colleagues to meet for a drink or two after work. As a matter of fact, the building where he lived isn't that far from here. Did he ever mention where he lived?"

She clasped her arms tight across her chest again. "I don't make it a habit to drink with the people I work with, Detective. As far as anything else you're suggesting…"

Jensen shrugged. "A busy single woman like

yourself, an attractive younger man in the same department... it wouldn't be unheard of for two people in that situation to hit it off."

Ms. Atchison shook her head decisively. "Like you said, I'm a single working mother of two teen boys. I have enough to do just taking care of the three of us, making sure there's food on the table and clothes on our backs. I can assure you, I don't have the time or the inclination to pursue a relationship on top of that. At least not right now."

"What about the other women in your department? Not all of them have the responsibilities you have. Did Nassar seem particularly friendly with any of them?"

"I'm sorry, if he was, I wasn't aware of it. Thinking back, my impression was that he spent the majority of his time in Ms. Walkowitz's office, working on the audit he was being paid to perform."

"But he did have some interactions with the staff. Did any of them take that the wrong way? Especially in view of his background, let's say?"

"You mean because he was Middle Eastern? But he wasn't the first person like that to work here. I mean, we have Mr. Fathy for instance, one of the other managers, who's from that part of the world too, and he's been here something like ten years. I don't doubt there were comments made by somebody–every large company has a few bad apples in it–but I don't recall hearing about any in particular."

"No complaints about outsiders coming in to take over?"

Ms. Atchison laughed a second time. "Because he was performing an audit? Detective, periodic audits are a normal procedure for a publicly-traded corporation like this one, whether they're carried out internally or by an independent contractor. There wouldn't be any reason for our employees to think it was out of the ordinary."

"But you knew better than that, didn't you?"

Ms. Atchison stared at the detective, without immediately responding, and Jensen continued calmly:

"This is no run-of-the-mill, random audit, and I know you're aware of that. How much did your supervisor tell you about the circumstances behind it?"

Ms. Atchison cleared her throat. "We–the four of us in the accounting department's management team– were told an irregularity had been discovered that affected a number of customer accounts, and the audit was needed to track it down and correct the problem."

"Just between us, why do you think the company called in an outside firm to perform the audit?"

She rolled her shoulders in an uneasy shrug. "It could be for any number of reasons. I suppose you want me to say it's because there was some fraud involved, maybe some wrongdoing on the part of one of the company's directors? Until I know otherwise, I prefer to assume it was just a mistake, and the board simply wanted a fresh pair of eyes to look over the accounts, someone who isn't familiar with the procedures we use and so would have an easier time spotting an error. I work hard at thinking the best of people, Detective, and not immediately concluding they're up to no good."

Jensen took the rebuke mildly, saying, "Unfortunately, I don't have that luxury. The people I deal with on a regular basis are usually guilty of something. Tell me about your normal routine here. You arrive for work around seven a.m.?"

"Yes, our hours are based around the New York Stock Exchange schedule. For the brokers, that's seven in the morning to a little after two in the afternoon. Our department, Accounting, is normally finished by four."

"And you live where?"

She blinked at him. "Is that important to your case, where I live? I mean, does it need to be made public?"

"Not necessarily. I'm just trying to get these things straight in my mind."

Ms. Atchison sighed, her arms clasped across her chest once more, and said, "Falshire West. It's a gated community on the southern edge of the city."

"On Falls Parkway, just a little off Tilton Avenue, isn't it? How long does it take you to drive there from here, normally?"

"About twenty-five minutes, maybe a bit less if traffic's good."

"I see. I think that covers everything for now, Ms. Atchison. Thank you. Would you ask Gerome Westbrook to step in here, please?"

The Southeast manager came in in his shirtsleeves, not bothering to slip on his suit jacket for the interview. He was the tallest of the four team leads in Accounting, on the slender side, with his thinning brown hair parted along the left and brushed across his scalp, and his long face bore a harassed expression.

When Detective Jensen explained the reason for the interview, Westbrook's response was curt.

"I don't see what you think I can tell you. Just because I met this young man, Nassar, when he began his audit, doesn't mean I know anything about him or his death. I was under the impression he was killed in some kind of hate crime. Isn't that the case?"

"It may be," Jensen said easily, "but before he was killed he received some threatening emails, and those were sent from one of the servers here at CanCorp. That tells me whoever killed him most likely works here–and possibly in the accounting department."

"I find that highly doubtful, but fine, go ahead. What do you want to know?"

"What was your impression of Kadeem Nassar? I realize you didn't speak to him much…"

"I didn't give him much thought, to be honest. If Janeen Walkowitz felt he was capable of doing the job, that was good enough for me. As far as I know, he came in, did his work, and kept to himself. I never heard of any issues between him and our staff."

"Were you surprised when you found out an outside audit was being conducted?"

Westbrook shrugged. "A company doesn't survive as long as this one has without encountering some difficulties along the way. There was some discrepancy in the accounts, and the board requested an external audit to find the problem and eliminate it. That's all there is to it. These sorts of audits do happen periodically in business."

"Did everyone take it as calmly as you did, though? After all, to have an outsider poking around and questioning company procedures, especially one with his background…"

"You mean, because he was Arabic, or whatever you want to call it? I don't pretend to know the politics of everyone who works in this department, but I can't believe any of them would be foolish enough to raise objections over something like that. This company abides by EEO standards. There's no place for anyone who spouts off racist or reactionary rhetoric."

"Very commendable. What about outside office hours? In some firms, the employees like to meet up after work for a drink or two. Did he ever do that?"

"I have no idea. It isn't a habit of mine, and hasn't been for a long time, so I couldn't tell you who does what when they're off the clock."

"The apartment building where he lived isn't all that far from here, as a matter of fact. Did you ever hear anyone mention that in conversation?"

"No," Westbrook said flatly.

"Tell me something about your usual routine. I understand the accounting department starts their day at seven a.m.?"

"All of our departments do. Our schedule is based around NYSE hours, and that's when the exchange opens in the morning."

"And the day ends when?"

"For us, four o'clock. That's our normal schedule. Some of the other departments, the brokers for instance, can generally finish earlier than that."

"How long does it normally take you to get home?"

Westbrook stared at the detective. "I don't see what that has to do with anything. All right, fine—a little over half an hour, in normal traffic."

"And you live where?"

"On Halsey Street, in Arlington." Westbrook held Jensen's gaze and added, "What's this all about? I had an investigator show up on my doorstep yesterday, asking questions about a traffic accident of some kind, and now you're asking me where I live. Was he from your office, too?"

Jensen shook his head and regarded the

businessman thoughtfully. "This is the first I've heard of it. But it could make someone wonder, what is it about you that has multiple people looking into your movements?"

Though it was hard for Amirah to see clearly over her monitor, Westbrook had gone ashen. "What is that supposed to mean?" he demanded. "Are you implying that I'm somehow involved in–in a racial attack? Do you know who I am, and who my family is? The very idea that I would stoop–"

Jensen held up his hand to stem the flow of words, and said blandly, "I suspect you're winding up to warn me that my superiors will be hearing about this. Don't waste your breath, Mr. Westbrook. My lieutenant has already been hearing from some important people, including the police commissioner, and they all want this case solved as soon as possible. So your best course would be to take a moment and rack your brain to see if there's anything you can think of that could possibly help us–and in the meantime, would you ask Mr. Fathy to step in here?"

Chapter 27

"Takis?" asked Hershey, holding out the purple-and-gold foil package.

Since Amirah was not particularly hungry, and since the IT tech had already had his fingers in the bag, she declined with a smile and a shake of her head and turned her attention back to the laptop screen.

Mahmud Fathy, the Southwest manager, entered the interview room with a determined dignity. He was shorter and stockier than Gerome Westbrook, with a squarish face and straight black hair that showed no trace of gray, and in his bowtie and elbow-patched suit he could have been anything from a head accountant to a law professor.

"Have a seat, Mr. Fathy," Jensen said. "Ms. Walkowitz explained why I'm here, I hope? We're investigating the murder of a young man named Kadeem Nassar, who was assisting her with a company audit, and since it appears his death was connected to the company in some way I'm talking to everyone in the accounting department, to see what information we can turn up."

Fathy sat with his hands clasped together on the tabletop, looking attentive but not relaxed. When he spoke his accent was heavy, betraying the fact that he had been in the States only a few years.

"I will answer questions if I can," he said simply,

"but I did not know this Nassar person. I have met him once, twice, possibly. The audit, it is not my affair."

"But you knew it was going on. Did it surprise you?"

"I do not understand."

Jensen said patiently, "We both know this isn't a routine audit. To call in an outside company to go over the books, that had to strike you as unusual."

"I repeat, it is not my affair. I do not concern myself with it."

"Okay. What was your impression of Nassar, generally speaking?"

Fathy shrugged, a quick jerk of his shoulders. "You are asking what I think about him? I did not think anything about him. He showed up on time every day and did his work, that is all I know. I am too busy with my own work to pay attention to everyone who is employed here."

"Would you have known if he had problems with any of the employees, in this department or any other department?"

This time the man's answer was a mere lifting of his hands in the air.

Jensen persevered. "Have you experienced any difficulties yourself with people in the company, seeing that you come from a similar background?"

Fathy sighed. "You are meaning have I been treated like I am suspicious character, maybe secretly terrorist? Always, in every place, there are some people who judge quickly, by what they see and not by the facts. This company is no different. But this does not mean I have complaints about my employment here. CanCorp is good company to work for, many good benefits."

"I see. Do you ever spend time with your colleagues outside office hours? Do you know if Kadeem Nassar did? Sometimes people like to stop somewhere for a drink or two, to socialize once they're off the clock…"

Fathy frowned. "Alcohol is *haram* in my culture. Not lawful. I would not spend my time in a place where it was taken."

"Did Nassar ever mention where he lived? It turns out it isn't very far from here."

The manager took a breath and said, "You have the idea we would be friends, because we are both Muslim, because our families come from the same part of the world? This is not correct. He was a Saudi, and half my age even; I am Egyptian. These are not the same."

"No, I don't suppose they are. Tell me about your usual routine here. You arrive at work around seven a.m.?"

"That is right."

"And leave when?"

"Usually I am finish by four o'clock."

"How long does it take you to drive home normally, would you say?"

"I do not know exactly. Maybe fifteen minutes, maybe twenty. I take the expressway east, then on to Upland Boulevard to the place where I live."

"What's the exact address?"

"It's 78 Woodlane Court. It is in the place called Glenn Pines."

"All right. Thank you, Mr. Fathy," Jensen said, making a note of the address. "Would you mind asking Mr. deWitt to come in here, please?"

Mahmud Fathy went out, with an expression reflecting bafflement at the exact purpose of the questions he had been asked, and a few minutes later the last of the accounting managers, Matt deWitt, strode in. He was of medium build, with prominent cheekbones and brown hair styled into a flat top look that was a good inch or so taller than regulation military length. He was jacketless like Westbrook had been, with his sleeves rolled to his elbows, and his manner was brusque.

"I hear you're asking questions about that auditor we had who was killed," he said as he sat down across from Jensen. "Don't see what any of us can tell you about it. The news report said he was killed in a robbery."

"There are some circumstances connected to the incident which we'd like to clear up," the detective answered noncommittally. "Did you interact with him much?"

"I met him when he started his audit a couple of months ago, that was about it."

"Were you surprised when you found out an audit was underway?"

DeWitt smirked briefly. "Somebody dropped the ball somewhere—that's what it meant to me. Or maybe tried to dip their hand into the accounts, I don't know. Either way, a company this size, an audit's bound to happen sooner or later. All I can say is, the issue isn't in my division. I run a tight unit."

"What was your impression of Nassar? Did he seem like the sort to rub people the wrong way?"

DeWitt crossed his arms and leaned back in his chair. "Well, whether he was trying to or not, he had to expect some kind of reaction, didn't he? An auditor from the outside, and someone from his background… They come over here and try to push their way into American businesses, and then they act surprised at the response they get."

"What response was that, exactly? And from who?"

"I don't want to get into pointing fingers, but it was a manager of another department, I'll say that much. The two of them got into it in the elevator one day and ended up shoving each other. They cooled off by the time the elevator got down to the lobby, I guess, because I never heard anything more than that, but that's where I'd start looking if I were you."

Jensen nodded. "I've heard something about the incident already. How about inside the accounting department? Did he ruffle any feathers there?"

DeWitt shrugged. "I don't know exactly. He seemed to spend all his time with our accounting head, working on the audit. Which is what he should have been doing, don't get me wrong. But he didn't go out of his way to make friends."

"He didn't spend any time with people from your department after hours? I know workmates sometimes like to have a drink or two and unwind after a long day."

DeWitt made a derisive sound. "Imagine him slumming with the likes of us! Besides it being against his religion or whatever, if you've talked to his family at all, you have to know he came from money. He didn't say it in so many words, but it was obvious from the way he dressed and acted."

"Did he ever say anything specific about himself or

his background? For example, where he lived?"

"He didn't discuss his life with anyone on my team, I can tell you that."

"Do you think he might have been reserved about himself because of being a Muslim? You've said already there are some in the company who have an issue with people of that kind…"

"We didn't treat him any differently than anybody else," deWitt said heatedly, uncrossing his arms and leaning forward abruptly. "Nobody can say we did. If he had thin skin about it, well, that was his problem, wasn't it?"

"Up to the point where someone put a knife in him," Jensen replied sourly. "Then it became my problem. Let's move on, Mr. deWitt. Tell me about your normal routine here in the accounting department. You get here at what time in the morning?"

"Seven a.m. A little before that, actually, but you know what I mean."

"And you generally leave when?"

"I'm out of here by three-thirty or four most days. Fridays can take a little longer, when I'm trying to wrap something up before the weekend."

"How long would you say the drive home takes you?"

DeWitt stared at him. "About fifteen minutes, give or take. What's that got to do with your case?"

"Just trying to get the little details straight. What route do you usually take?"

"I live in Holiday Hills, on the other side of the river–902 Skyline Drive, in case you want to write that down–so I get right onto the expressway, off at the Archer Avenue exit, and straight on to my subdivision.

Anything else?"

"No, I think that's it for now. Thank you, Mr. deWitt."

Matt deWitt went out of the interview room with a frown, and a minute or two later, Jensen followed, probably to take a break and get himself something from the nearest vending machine. Amirah, whose tailbone was urging her to move around as well, rose and put away her earpiece and receiver. With a quick thanks to Hershey, she stepped out into the hallway and called her husband.

"Hon? Detective Jensen just finished with the last of the accounting managers... No, none of them said anything that could be proof of the murderer's identity. He didn't even seem to get close to the right questions. I think the police are still a step or two behind us, and... Yes. Definitely... Will you? I'll talk to Janeen Walkowitz, and let her know the plan, and if she can get hold of her boss... Okay. I'll wait for your call. Love you."

Amirah headed down the corridor toward the elevators with a distinct energy in her step. Detective Jensen's sessions with the four managers might not have yielded any significant results, but that only meant it was Gates and Gates' turn at bat.

Chapter 28

On the polished black surface of the long table, four new yellow notepads sat in a row, with four new pens placed neatly alongside them. Ms. Walkowitz glanced briefly at the table again and stepped to the door to admit the accounting managers.

Out beyond the windows that covered the far wall the noonday sky was a bright blue, and in the distance, to the northwest, the mirrored surface of Lake Womack suggested laughter and relaxation. Here, in the main conference room on the forty-first floor of Canfield Tower, there was not even so much as a smile.

Amirah Gates had a craving for another cup of coffee–except that she was nervous enough as it was, and more caffeine would probably have given her fits.

There had been a succession of phone calls after she had ended her conversation with her husband. Mason had telephoned Lieutenant Raymonde to explain their idea and had gotten an unenthusiastic response. Amirah meanwhile had described the plan to Janeen Walkowitz, who had called Jerald Canfield and outlined it to him; he in turn had called his friend the police commissioner, who completed the circle by getting the lieutenant on the phone and instructing him to give the plan a try–with the expectation, between them, that it would lead nowhere and free up the police to pursue their investigation without further interference.

The managers filed in and took their seats on the side of the table holding the notepads, as the accounting head directed. None of them looked particularly happy, if for no other reason than this arrangement was cutting into their lunch hour. Mahmud Fathy was dour; Samantha Atchison's baby-blue eyes were wide and her complexion pale; Gerome Westbrook's long face was drawn and a touch resentful; and Matt deWitt shifted his crewcut head from side to side suspiciously.

As the four got settled Amirah and Mason stepped forward alongside Ms. Walkowitz on the opposite side of the table, while Lieutenant Raymonde stayed toward the back of the room, his hands clasped loosely behind him, flanked by Detective Jensen and a uniformed patrolman no one had bothered to introduce.

"I want to say first of all," Ms. Walkowitz began, "that we appreciate this is an inconvenience for you, and we wouldn't have dragged you in here again except under the most serious of circumstances. You all had to take time out of your schedules this morning to talk with Detective Jensen about the Nassar case, but there has been more going on than you're probably aware of. This young woman, who I previously introduced to you as merely a temp in our department, is actually a private investigator hired to find Kadeem Nassar's killer. She and her husband have explained that they've been able to narrow down their list of suspects to one of four people, and they believe they can identify the person involved by means of a simple test. I assured them that the four of you would be willing to do whatever is needed to clear this matter up."

The speech produced varied results. Fathy narrowed his eyes and stared at the three of them. Ms.

Atchison's eyes got wider, if that was possible. Westbrook muttered in disbelief. DeWitt growled, "You're saying you think one of us is a murderer?"

Lieutenant Raymonde cleared his throat. "You should be aware, this is not an official arrangement by any means. We are only here as observers. You are not obligated to take part, and if any of you feel you need to consult a lawyer before answering questions or complying with any other requests, that's your right."

"Although," Mason said quickly, "as I pointed out to one of your colleagues earlier this week, the upper management of CanCorp is fully aware of our investigations, and a refusal to cooperate might not look very good in their eyes."

"Fine. Let's get on with it," Westbrook said. "I've got work to do."

"What we want you to do is very simple," Amirah said. "On the pads in front of you, we want you to print–in all capital letters–the words 'Die Arab.' That's it. This is the message that was left on the victim's car by his killer."

"You've got to be kidding me," grumbled deWitt, but picked up the provided pen along with the others.

It took only a few seconds, and Amirah and Mason circled the table to view the results over the managers' shoulders. There was little to differentiate between the writing samples. Printing is printing, after all, and there was no real way to compare what was in front of them with the letters that had been scratched into the side of Kadeem Nassar's car.

Amirah looked chagrined, and turned to her husband. "Do you think…? What we discussed, I mean?"

He nodded, and they came back around the table. "I'm afraid that wasn't as conclusive as we would have liked," he told the four executives. "If you'll bear with us, there's one more thing we'd like to try, and it should only take a few minutes. If we could have all of you come around to this side of the table and simply empty your pockets–and in your case, Ms. Atchison, your purse as well…"

The managers glared and sighed and rolled their eyes. DeWitt demanded, "Is this really necessary? It's a waste of time. I don't believe for one moment you have any evidence one of us was involved, and besides, we have rights…"

Ms. Walkowitz, who had only received the briefest outline of what Mason and Amirah had intended to do, looked embarrassed. "Please, Matt. I realize it's an imposition, but the sooner we get this over with, the happier everyone will be. And as Mr. Gates said, it'll only take a minute or two."

The four suspects complied grudgingly. Ms. Walkowitz stepped back out of the way as they began to pile the contents of their pockets on the glossy tabletop. Mason took up a position at the far end of the table, where he could see everything that was happening, while Amirah hovered around the managers, leaning past them to poke at their belongings and completely disregarding their personal space.

She started at the opposite end of the table from where her husband was standing, browsing through Mr. Westbrook's things and then Ms. Atchison's. When she came to the third manager, Mahmud Fathy, she stretched her hand out to the heap in front of him and then stopped.

"What's this?"

Under her hand was a man's watch with a pale leather band and a dark face bearing narrow Roman numerals. It was clearly not Fathy's usual wristwatch. That was still attached to his wrist, a rugged metallic item with a large digital display.

She looked up at him, her hazel eyes large. "That looks like Kadeem Nassar's watch. How did you get this, Mr. Fathy?"

He stared back at her and said loudly, "This is lie! You are liar! I have never see this watch before today!"

"What do you mean?" she responded innocently. "It's right here, among your belongings…"

Fathy's face darkened. The others in the room went quiet as he stormed on.

"You cannot put the blame on me with this! This is trick. You are trying to make me responsible for this man's death. It is not so! It is you. You put this watch here for everyone to see!"

"Me?"

Amirah's ingenuous tone only spurred on his anger.

"Yes, you! You are liar! My hands have not touched this watch. Make the test, I insist. Everyone will see then, only your hands have touched it. It is not even the watch of the dead man, is it? Tell the truth! It is all fake, to try to make me guilty!"

To the surprise of just about everyone else in the room, Amirah dropped her head and looked up at him sheepishly.

"You're right, Mr. Fathy. It–it was a crazy thing to do. And it didn't work. Why not? What gave me away?"

He snorted in derision. "This watch, it is all wrong. You cannot fool anyone with this. It is fake. The dead man, the accountant who work here, the watch he wore is white, not leather like this."

In the silence that followed that statement, Lieutenant Raymonde stepped forward from his place at the back of the room.

"Would you mind repeating that, Mr. Fathy?" he asked quietly.

Amirah lifted her head with a grimly triumphant expression. "You're right, Mr. Fathy. Again. When Kadeem Nassar was killed, he was wearing a Fitbit watch with a white band. But that was the watch he wore to the gym, not the one he wore here to the office. The only way you could have known about that watch is if you saw it on his wrist, while you had your arm around his throat, stabbing him to death."

The man's eyes blazed as he realized what he had said, and how she had maneuvered him. His hand flew to his shirt pocket and emerged with what appeared to be a black ballpoint pen. With a quick twist of his wrists, it came apart into two pieces. The piece in his left hand ended in a small, keen blade.

He lunged at Amirah, enraged, as she threw up her arms. The executives scattered. The patrolman yanked his pistol from its holster and tried to get a clear line of fire.

Mason moved.

Later, whenever he was prompted to tell the story, he always started by admitting that what he did next was a foolish thing to do. Fathy could easily have swung around to face him, and that razor-sharp knife could have wound up buried in Mason's own heart. But his wife was in danger, and at the moment that was his only consideration.

He planted his left foot against the beveled edge of the conference table and pushed off. He left the floor at an ungainly angle, sailed through the space between them, and crashed into the accounting manager. They went down in a tangle as Amirah jumped to the side, and the knife flew out of Fathy's hand and bounced across the tan carpet.

They rolled back and forth, each trying to get an arm free to take a solid swing at the other, and banged up against the water cooler next to the patrolman, who still had his pistol in his hands.

Finally, Mason levered himself across the other man, his knee pinning down Fathy's left bicep, and slammed his fist into his jaw, once, twice.

"Enough, Gates, enough," said Lieutenant Raymonde. "We'll take it from here."

The patrolman holstered his weapon and rolled Fathy over onto his stomach to handcuff him. Mason got to his feet stiffly, dusting himself off, and turned to face the senior officer.

"Well, you saw all that for yourself, Lieutenant. He's your man." Mason pointed to the knife shining wickedly on the patterned carpet. "And that, I very much suspect, is the murder weapon."

Chapter 29

"You want some more *mutabbaq*, sweetheart?"

Mason bobbed his head happily and Amirah slid two more pieces of the savory stuffed bread onto his plate as he held it up.

Saturday evening had finally arrived, and the anniversary party for Faisal and Basma Bukhari was in full swing. The restaurateur, ensconced at the head of the fully-extended table, beamed down its length at his wife, his four daughters and their husbands, all chatting away merrily. Everything was arranged to his satisfaction: instead of a reception in some lavish rented hall, the gathering was being held at home, the natural place for family; instead of a hired band, Middle Eastern folk music wafted from an iPod dock in one corner; instead of an expensive and overly-rich cake, traditional Saudi desserts lined a sideboard to his left, *qatayef* and *knafeh* and *muhallebi*.

"So it was all a trick?" asked Amirah's sister Sumayyah, leaning toward them across the table.

"Yes," Amirah said. Mason had willingly let her recount the story of their investigation to her family, while he sat back and enjoyed the food that had been prepared. "Actually, both of the first steps were tricks, to lull Mahmud Fathy into a false ease. We knew there was no way of matching up anybody's printing with the message scratched into Kadeem Nassar's car; there just isn't any science that can do that. After that effort 'failed' he was sure to think we didn't have anything solid on him. Then I had them all empty their pockets and pretended to hunt through their belongings, which just made him think we were stumbling around in the dark more. So when I slipped Kadeem's wristwatch, which I'd gotten from his sister the day before, out of my pocket and into the pile in front of him, it caught him off guard. Enough for him to blurt out a description of the watch Kadeem actually was wearing when he was killed."

"You don't think he'll try to fight it?" asked Sumayyah's husband. "Claiming entrapment or something like that?"

"I don't think so," Mason answered. "Multiple witnesses can testify to his admission of 'guilty knowledge' relating to Kadeem's death. The stolen funds have been traced to bank accounts he set up, and with the additional charges of first-degree murder and attempted murder, he'll be going away for quite a few years."

"And he stole how much?" asked Sumayyah. "About two million, two and a half?"

"In the long term, he was hoping for much more," said Amirah. "He was periodically investing part of the stolen money in high-yield bonds, and with the returns from that and what he would be getting from his company retirement account, he was potentially looking at around double the money he stole–say five million or so–when it was all over."

From Mason's right her sister Yara leaned into the conversation. "And how did you know he was the one? What gave him away before the slip about the wristwatch?"

"For my part," Mason said, "it was his address. The subdivision he lives in borders the mall where the killer used the credit cards he took from Kadeem's wallet. In fact, the back entrance to the mall connects directly to his street. That particular mall was out of the way for the other three suspects. Two of them live on the southern fringe of Cathedral City, far in the opposite direction, and the third would've had to pass the exit to his home and double back afterward, and I couldn't see any reason for that." He shrugged. "It wasn't positive proof, but it was a good indication, especially coupled with what Amirah realized."

His wife swallowed quickly as they looked back in her direction. "At CanCorp, I was told Mahmud Fathy didn't speak English very well, and used a computer program that translated his emails and other work from Arabic. When I heard that I remembered the second threatening email Kadeem received, and the odd way it was worded. 'You will die, you son of the dog.' The police thought that last part was just a typo for a certain common profanity, but I'm sure you can recall hearing it as a kid from *baba* and the other older men the same as me…"

"*Ibn al Kalb*," murmured Faisal Bukhari, who was following their conversation with half his attention. "The old traditional insult."

"Yes, *baba*. Exactly. I put that together with the fact Mr. Fathy shopped from a self-defense company, and would've had access to the kind of unusual knife used to kill Kadeem, and I was certain he was the guilty party. Then all that was left was to catch him."

"And what was this knife?" asked Yara's husband.

"I don't understand. Some sort of ballpoint pen?"

"It was meant to look like a pen," Amirah said. "That way he could carry it on him without anyone suspecting. When it was twisted apart there was a two-inch blade inside."

"Oh, my poor daughter," lamented Amirah's mother. "That horrible man very nearly killed you– twice! Such a dangerous occupation for you."

Faisal, who had on more than one occasion voiced his opinion that the investigative business was no place for a woman, wisely refrained from adding his two cents' worth to the exchange.

"I swear, Mrs. Bukhari," Mason protested, "most of the cases our agency handles are a lot less exciting."

"But occasionally entertaining," said Amirah. "Tell them about Richard Daniel Reeves and his attempt at swindling Supreme Insurance."

Mason gave a sharp laugh and took his turn as storyteller, briefly describing the insurance fraud case and ending with Reeves' confession on video.

"You can't be serious," Sumayyah said. "He actually admitted the whole thing in front of you?"

"Yes, after agreeing to let me film him." Mason laughed. "The average criminal is not, generally speaking, the brightest crayon in the box. Granted, he had no way of knowing I understood Arabic, but even if he was speaking something like Klingon, he should've suspected I'd eventually find someone to translate it for me."

"So what do you think?" asked Sumayyah's husband. "Will this be a new field for you, solving crimes the police can't seem to get a grip on?"

Mason shook his head, while Amirah raised her

eyebrows puckishly and said nothing. "Kadeem Nassar's murder was a special instance. If we hadn't had the head of a major corporation as one of our clients, I don't think we would have gotten as far as we did as quickly as we did. Not to mention that the police generally frown on outside agencies poking their noses into their bailiwick. No, I predict in the future we'll stick to our usual field of investigation–insurance cases and other types of fraud, security work, and so on. Besides which…"

He trailed off and looked at his wife.

Basma Bukhari clapped her hands together, cutting through the various conversations. "Aziza, will you help me, please? I think it is time for dessert."

The two of them rose and picked up platters from the sideboard to transfer them onto the table, while the others rearranged dishes to make room.

"Should we tell them?" Mason asked Amirah under his breath.

"Why not?" she replied. "Now's as good a time as any."

He took a deep breath, and pitching his voice over the clattering of tableware, announced: "We're pregnant."

Her mother and sister stopped still, holding the trays of sweets, and then the room erupted in joyous congratulations. Faisal and Basma beamed at the news of another grandchild being added to their family.

"I suspect," Mason murmured to his wife, grinning, "we just upstaged dessert."

## A word about the author...

Darin and Sarah Fortner have been happily married for ten years and live in west-central Indiana, where they are the proud parents of an adorably affectionate red tabby. They enjoy watching a variety of TV shows and movies, especially mysteries (although Sarah tends to solve the mystery too quickly!). They also enjoy puzzles and games of all sorts and spending time with loved ones. In addition they serve as volunteer ministers in their community.

Darin has held a variety of jobs over the years, primarily in customer service. From an early age he has delighted in exploring the world of books and has written stories to amuse himself. In recent years he has self-published two historical mystery novels detailing the investigations of a WWI veteran in South Carolina in the 1930s.

Sarah has an Associate of Applied Science degree in Office Administration, and has held positions in fields ranging from retail grocery to mental health. She is a master at learning and using different kinds of computer programs. She also shares a love of card games with various family members and friends.

Thank you for purchasing
this publication of The Wild Rose Press, Inc.

For questions or more information
contact us at
info@thewildrosepress.com.

The Wild Rose Press, Inc.
www.thewildrosepress.com